DEATH GETS INTO THE ACT

HARRY COLDERWOOD—A once well-known magician, he could perform to perfection 175 tricks and illusions, but the reality was his magic career was fading fast. Now murder had shuffled his cards and left him a hand full of jokers...danger...and death.

WANDA MORROW—The pretty widow who said she wanted to find out who killed her husband. She had the money to hire Harry, but did she expect some particularly personal service as part of the bargain?

DR. RANDY PESCATORE—A shrink with a talent for showing up in suspicious places. Did he push Mr. Morrow into one last primal scream...or was his interest in murder purely professional?

LOGAN ZOLLER—The dead man's partner in the book business. He was an expert in rare editions, but did he also specialize in writing Morrow's final chapter?

JOYCE GILDEA—A very blonde, very beautiful, and very available reporter. She has a nose for news and bedroom eyes for a man with a magic touch.

SLEIGHTLY MURDER

PATRICK A. KELLEY

AVON
PUBLISHERS OF BARD, CAMELOT, DISCUS AND FLARE BOOKS

AVON BOOKS
A division of
The Hearst Corporation
1790 Broadway
New York, New York 10019

Copyright © 1985 by Patrick A. Kelley
Published by arrangement with the author
Library of Congress Catalog Card Number: 84-091238
ISBN: 0-380-89511-0

First Avon Printing, April 1985

AVON TRADEMARK REG. U.S. PAT. OFF. AND IN OTHER COUNTRIES, MARCA REGISTRADA, HECHO EN U.S.A.

Printed in the U.S.A.

WFH   10   9   8   7   6   5   4   3   2   1

Special thanks to the staff of our local public library for their generous assistance.

To my wife, Marilyn—who *is* magic, beyond all belief.

CHAPTER ONE

Working on a holiday is a drag. Getting fired on a holiday is even worse.

To some, Halloween may not be much of a holiday. But to us magicians, it has always been a special day. Houdini even chose the thirty-first of October to make his final escape from this world. I've often wondered, during my more cynical moments, whether or not his death was the ultimate cheap publicity stunt.

Yet, holiday or not, here I was, pacing back and forth on a cold, ill-lit street corner in a Pennsylvania town that three days ago I had never heard of. Every time a car or pedestrian passed, I tried not to look suspicious. But a man wearing a jogging suit and doing anything other than jogging looks, well, suspicious. Particularly if he is smoking cigarettes with the relish of a confirmed nonfitness addict.

I silently gave Morrow another ten minutes.

After all, they were *his* ghosts, not mine.

I littered the sidewalk with yet another cigarette butt. I jammed my hands as best I could into my tiny jacket pockets. The designer must have pictured the buyer of the jacket gobbling up mile after mile, with his arms doing nothing but pumping like a locomotive. The pockets were too small for hands. You could not carry anything bigger than, say, an ID in them. The ID would come in handy when you were found at the crest of some humongous hill. Dead. Of a heart attack.

Down the block, a squat lady with her head swathed in a bandanna shuffled toward me. Her shoes made dull clop-clops on the sidewalk brick. The clops slowed as she neared me. She crossed the street and passed me on the opposite side. I probably fit the description of every convenience store stickup man in the area for the past six months.

The vacant storefront behind me did nothing to shield me from the wind. No matter where I stood, the night chill found me.

Where the hell are you, Morrow?

I turned and put my face close to the filthy window of the store. It had once been a sign shop. In the dimness, I discerned a crude wooden table with cans and jars of paint atop it. Stacked against the wall were signs and posters of various sizes advertising a host of businesses and events. The owner should have invested a little less in paint and a little more on a good dictionary. I never trust any business that cannot spell what they are selling.

The wind revved up again. The dampness inside my running suit made it worse. I had misjudged the distance from my motel, figuring it as only a mile and a half. I was off by only a couple of miles. My initially confident running style had quickly eroded to a walk/jog, relying a great deal more on the walk. I blamed my bad wind on the cigarettes. I should have taken a cab.

Five more minutes, Morrow. No more.

The corner street lamp was dark, a victim of either neglect or some kid with a good aim. Over half the houses on the avenue were dark. Maybe these people go to bed early. Or maybe a lot of them have moved out.

About a block away, a car started up. In a few moments it glided into view. Its headlights were off. It eased through the intersection, ignoring the stop sign, and pulled over to the curb in front of me. Several people—I couldn't tell how many—were inside.

The car sat, silent, for a long minute. My hands contracted into fists inside my jacket pockets. You often hear about surgeons' paranoia over the safety of their hands. Professional magicians fear hand injury even more. Surgeons can recuperate in their big homes, sipping expensive drinks, watching large-screen TVs, and being pampered by maids. Magicians, unless you are a Copperfield or a Henning, have little to look forward to except bills, musty hotel rooms, more bills, and second-rate medical care. It is not that I have never found an excuse to use my fists a time or two. But I have always regretted my impulsiveness later.

"Get over here."

The voice came from the open front window of the car.

"Morrow?" I said.

I must have said the secret "woid," but no duck came down, and I won no jackpot. They all barreled out of the car as though I had thrown a live grenade into it. There were three of them, two in uniform.

"Police. Hold it."

The two in uniform handled me with the firm sureness of wild-animal trainers. In no time they had me leaning against their unmarked car.

"You guys better fix those lights. Never pass state inspection that way."

They patted me down in every pattable place. It amused me that they only gave passing attention to my sleeves. Talk to any kid, and he will tell you that magicians do *every* trick with something hidden up the sleeves.

"Clean, Sarge."

"While you were frisking, you didn't happen to notice if I had any constitutional rights left, did you?"

"All gone," the one in plain clothes said. "No ID, Ed?"

Ed shook his head. They let me stand up straight again. I kneaded the cramps out of my upper arms. Leaning on a cop car looks easy, but it is hell on your triceps.

"Name, please?"

I told the sergeant.

"Address and occupation?"

I told him. And winced.

"You do *what?*"

Ed came to my rescue. "I think he's telling the truth, Sarge."

At Ed's request, I removed my watch cap so he could study my face.

"Yep, that's him. My wife and I took the boy to the mall yesterday. He's the guy that did the tricks. He even made a little sausage doggie out of a balloon for Billy.

"Hey, you used to be on TV, didn't you? How come you don't do that trick anymore where you make that Chevy pickup disappear? Or that one where the lady disappears out of the cannon?"

For the hundredth time in the past couple of years, I answered those questions. I told him it was due to state fire regulations, and I think he believed me.

"I'm tickled to hear that little Billy liked his balloon doggie," the sergeant said. He was in his midforties and wore new blue jeans and a plaid shirt. Even though he had over a dozen years on me, he looked more physically fit. And *I* was the one in the exercise getup. His hooded poplin jacket was unzipped, and he seemed oblivious to the night air's sting.

"Colderwood. Nice name for a magician. That your real name? I see. You should change your first name, though. Harry is too dull for a professional magician."

"Houdini liked it fine. And Blackstone and Lorayne didn't do too badly by it, either."

"Who's Harry Lorayne?"

"The memory expert. He's been on TV."

"Must have slipped my mind." He chuckled dryly at his own joke. "Of course, I never saw you on TV, either, but Ed apparently has. Vanished a Chevy pickup, did you? Now, how in the world did you—? Oh, I forgot. You magicians have a code of ethics, don't you? 'Never reveal a secret.' Right? Crooks and thieves and murderers have a code of ethics too. It's something like 'Keep your mouth shut around cops.' That's too similar to your code for my liking.

"Cops have a code too. In fact, we've got codes and rules and regulations and restrictions coming out our asses. Good thing I never take much stock in codes. Right, Bernie? Right, Ed?"

Bernie and Ed nodded.

A hardness descended over the sergeant's face. He was ready for work.

"Mr. Colderwood, answer just one question and we'll leave you alone. We'll even apologize for coming on you like storm troopers. What the fuck are you doing on this street corner?"

"Jogging."

"With no ID? A very ill-advised practice. What if you had a heart attack? Your body could go unclaimed for days. Even weeks."

"The thought occurred to me. Believe me."

"Your choice of colors is pretty stupid, too. That shade of blue is as dark as Bernie's uniform. So's your hat. Oncoming traffic would have a hell of a time spotting you."

"Especially when they don't have their lights on."

"You're a funny one, Colderwood. You go out for a midnight run in a bad section of a strange town. You forget to carry identification, but you do have the presence of mind to bring your cigarettes and Bic lighter. What chapter in *The Complete Book of Running* covers the most efficient way to run and smoke at the same time?"

I shrugged.

"And just look at you now. You're shivering. If I were out running tonight, I'd want to keep moving, not mope around on a street corner for twenty minutes."

So they had been staked out up the street.

"I had to get my second wind."

"I hope you got it. You just might need it. When we pulled up, you said something to us. Refresh our memory. What did you say?"

"Sorry. I don't remember."

What did you do, Morrow?

"My memory's better than yours, Colderwood. You said one word: Morrow. Right, Bernie?"

Bernie nodded.

"How about you, Ed? Is that what you heard?"

Ed hesitated. He was a tainted witness. After all, I had made a balloon sausage doggie for little Billy. He finally nodded. So much for buying testimony.

"Mr. Morrow couldn't make it tonight, Colderwood. So the three of us, you might say, are his emissaries."

The sergeant took a scrap of notepaper from his shirt pocket and unfolded it.

"Sixty-five miles per hour," he said, reading from the paper.

"What's that?"

"That's how fast Morrow was going."

"What the hell was he driving?"

"Nothing. I figured this out on the way over here. You took high school physics, didn't you? That's how fast Morrow's body was going when it finally hit the pavement."

He refolded the paper and tucked it back inside his pocket.

"It really fucked up his posture, Colderwood."

"When did this happen?"

"Let's go down to City Hall and talk about it over a cup of coffee."

"When did it happen?"

"Last night. You know the big parking garage downtown? In the past couple of years it's become quite a popular site for jumpers. I think the city should charge extra when people use the place for something other than parking."

"What time?"

"About one o'clock this morning. Hey, you're really shivering now. Let's get in the car and warm up. Come on."

"So it happened on Halloween."

"Huh? Oh, yeah. It was after midnight, so that makes it the thirty-first."

"No chance it was all just a cheap publicity stunt?"

"What did you say?"

"Nothing."

He held the back door open for me, and I slid in without another word. Sometimes you just do not feel like fighting City Hall.

CHAPTER TWO

My stay in Bayorvale had promised to be brief and pleasant. It was neither. My agent had booked me into the Vale Mall for a three-day engagement that was to culminate with an afternoon show on Sunday. Halloween.

Working the shopping mall circuit was not the pinnacle of my career. My agent had booked me into such entertainment meccas as the Nittany Valley Mall, the Rolling Hills Mall, and the Beaver Valley Mall. Why do they choose such bucolic names for these glass-and-concrete monsters?

My mall act would never rate a *Variety* review. But I could look in the mirror (usually cracked, depending on the motel I was staying at) in the morning and tell myself that I was still a paid entertainer.

But my career reached a new low when I drove my van full of magic equipment into the town of Bayorvale. Fifteen minutes before the start of my first show on Friday, my assistant informed me that she was quitting. She planned to stay on awhile in Bayorvale, sharing an apartment with the manager of the electronics store in the Vale Mall. Suddenly the name Radio Shack took on a new dimension for me.

To say the least, my performance foundered. I had to root frantically through the trunks and fish out all the props my assistant normally waltzed onstage to hand me. I eliminated all the tricks that required her to set up. I eliminated my big finish, the Zig Zag Illusion. In that illusion, my assistant would walk into a big box, and I would then slide out the middle section of the box. It looked like her entire abdomen had moved sideways a foot. Quite astonishing. I wanted to do the same thing with that Radio Shack guy's midsection, only without the benefit of a box.

There were only three tricks left that I could do by myself. I breezed through them in ten minutes and filled the remaining twenty-five minutes with card tricks.

I wish it were the worst show I have ever done. It was not. My last performance on Saturday night was even worse.

Bayorvale is located about twenty miles south of Johnstown. Johnstown was suffering from a half-decade bout with heavy unemployment, with no relief in sight. Bayorvale was faring only slightly better. Crowds at the Vale Mall were thin, with shoppers not spending as much as a few years before. Some spent nothing at all. Perhaps that is why the Mall Merchants Association advertised my magic show the way they did.

They could have changed the name of the place to the Chapter Eleven Mall. Many of the shopping areas had Closed signs posted on the iron gates blocking their entrances. Several others were staging stock-liquidation sales.

The *Bayorvale Dispatch* ran a half-page ad that heralded my act as a "Night of fright. Not recommended for the weak of heart. Girls, find out whether your boyfriends are mice or men! The Colderwood Magic Show is a perfect ten on the Frightometer!" It looked as if my ad copy had been mixed up with that of a sorority house slasher flick. Somehow the mall people had assumed I would perform a spook show.

Theatres in the thirties, forties, and up until the middle 1950s featured spook shows to promote horror movies. They were live magic productions that emphasized ghostly effects. They rarely lived up to their spectacular ad campaigns, but the audiences rarely cared. It was a different era. Only one magician, Aldo Gastini, presented a spook show close to the quality of the full-evening programs of Blackstone or Thurston.

When I complained about the false advertising, the president of the Merchants Association informed me that they had been assured by my agent that I could do a spook show. When I tried to explain that I could not change my basic act overnight, he politely requested I perform the Vanishing Chevy Pickup that he had seen me do on TV a few years back. I politely consented, as long as they provided me with fifty thousand dollars, a twenty-man crew, special lighting, and two weeks of rehearsal. He politely threw my ass out of his office.

So, with no assistant and audiences that showed up expecting to be scared silly, I hobbled through three shows on Friday and Saturday, using only ropes, linking rings, balloon animals, cards, and my built-in, lifetime supply of chutzpah. The Bayorvale audiences really got into the Halloween spirit, judging by the number of times they used the word "boo."

As I said, the last show on Saturday was the nadir. My performing platform was positioned in the worst possible area of the mall—in front of Zippy's Video Arcade. The bips and boings of disintegrating space fleets and galaxies were nonstop. The din abated slightly during my performances only because half the arcade denizens would vacate their command posts and come out to the mall area to catch each show. They hooted, heckled, and jeered me during each trick. I had developed a local cult following. None of my standard heckler stoppers dampened their spirits. I learned what it must have felt like to be a college administrator with a bullhorn in the 1960s.

Even the elementary school kids picked up bad habits from their elders. It was disheartening to see a cute eight-year-old girl, clutching an E.T. doll, cup her hand to her mouth and shout, "You suck!"

The spook show advertising and the heckling, along with the repeated playing of Perry Como Christmas songs and blaring P.A. announcements about illegally parked cars, all caused something to snap inside me. It happened right after one of the arcade kids interrupted my show to ask why I wore the same mangy tuxedo all the time.

I learned very early in my performing career two cardinal rules of magicianship. Number One is never, under any circumstances, call any member of your audience an asshole. Rule Two states that if you break Rule Number One, never do it while your agent is in the audience.

I did. And he was.

I did not notice Marlon Tate until I was repacking my equipment. The crowd had dispersed, leaving Marlon where he had been standing for the whole show. His arms were crossed, and the ubiquitous cigarette jutted from the corner of his mouth. Wearing a denim work shirt with two flapped breast pockets, he looked more like an auto me-

17

chanic than an entertainment agent. When the crowd was completely gone, he walked slowly up to the edge of the platform.

"Marlon. Nice to see you. How was the drive from Pittsburgh? Wow, this platform is a little shaky. Maybe you can talk them into fixing it for the Sunday shows."

He nodded, and I went back to resetting the equipment. After a minute of smoking and staring at me, he said, "Where's your assistant?"

I told him.

"Why all the card tricks when you've got a truckload of equipment?"

I told him.

"Why were they booing?"

I told him.

"Why did you call that one kid an asshole?"

I told him.

And then he fired me.

"Marlon, what about tomorrow's shows? What are you going to do about the next three months' worth of shows?"

"You've been replaced."

"By who?"

"Him."

He pointed to a skinny teenager with big ears who was leaning against the wall by Zippy's Video Arcade. The kid flashed me a mocking smile. He had been one of the jeering arcade patrons that helped ruin every show. That explained why they knew how every trick was done.

"I've been in town all day," Marlon said. "When I got word you were screwing up, I did some scouting around. The kid's got a reputation. They say he's a natural."

"For what? Cub Scouts and fire hall Christmas parties? You sure he's old enough to drive?"

"He's got a driver's license and a high school diploma. Plus, he says he can do any trick you're doing, only *twice* as well. Judging from that last sterling performance, I don't doubt him.

"He's got a whole attic full of props to supplement the equipment I've already bought for this tour. If he doesn't work out, you can stay for a few more shows until I rustle up another replacement. You can give me the van keys when you're done packing up here. Lucky they didn't

18

throw anything hard," he said, picking up a crumpled paper cup.

It was one of many articles of trash my admiring audience had thrown at me. Didn't crowds used to toss jelly beans onstage for the Beatles? Or was that for Ronald Reagan?

"Forget it, Tate. I'm calling it a night right now. Here are your keys," I said, dropping them on the floor. "You and your new recruit can strike the set. Let's get square before I leave, though. You owe me three weeks' pay. Plus a refund of three hundred fifty bucks of the five hundred I kicked in to pay for the Zig Zag."

"You're dreaming, Colderwood. Consider yourself lucky if you don't end up in court over this."

"Oh, I might end up in court. Criminal court. For assault."

I grabbed the mike stand and wielded it like a club. The base weighed over twenty pounds. I didn't care what part of Tate I dented.

Before I got close to him, a strong set of hands clamped around my left arm. Another person pried the stand from my grip. Both these fellows wore uniforms and hats, but they weren't cops. They were mall security men, armed with nightsticks, jumbo walkie-talkies, and very baggy pants. Remembering my well-publicized physical encounters with my last two agents, Tate was not taking any chances. He probably slipped the guards a couple of tens to help him out.

The storm inside me abated as quickly as it had risen.

"You guys can back off, now. I'm not going to hurt him. People like Tate are immune to head injuries, anyway. When I get the circulation back in my arms, I'm clearing out."

Under their wary eye, I packed up all the apparatus I could rightly call mine. There was not much, and it all fit into an attaché case. The most valuable item was a set of Chinese linking rings once owned by the legendary Dai Vernon.

The rings jingled in the case as I descended the platform steps. I breezed past Tate, totally ignoring him, and blended into the crowd of Saturday night shoppers. Well, I blended in as well as a man can when wearing a tuxedo in a blue-collar shopping mall.

19

I chuckled, realizing that I had completed yet one more step downward in what I was now calling my "reverse comeback bid." Yet, within twenty minutes someone made me another professional offer. Professional, that is, if you consider exorcism a profession.

I was sitting in the back corner of one of the mall's slower fast-food joints, nursing a cup of tea and chewing on one of those cardboard-tasting hamburgers advertised as tasting so much better than the cardboard-tasting burgers served by the competition. I had a napkin tucked in my collar to protect my tux shirt from dripping condiments. I accidentally dipped my ruffled sleeve in my tea anyway.

"This seat taken?"

I looked around the restaurant. Barely half the seats were filled. "No, be my guest," I said to the stranger.

The man took off his topcoat and slid into my booth, across the table from me. He was a few years younger than me, certainly no older than thirty. He wore his hair short but well styled, brushing it back on the sides and top. He wore a camel-color blazer and no tie. The lapels of his shirt splayed awkwardly over the lapels of his coat. His moustache was wide, emphasizing the sallow, unfed look of his face.

I assumed he was a local magician. After almost every show someone comes up and introduces himself as a brother practitioner of the art. Many professional magicians shun amateurs. I never ignore them because I almost always learn something. Often twelve-year-old kids demonstrate tricks and sleights that are totally new to me.

I was wrong about this man. He was no magician. He pulled a newspaper clipping from his coat pocket and slid it across the table. It was almost as yellow as the tabletop.

"Are you Colderwood, the guy in this picture?"

"Yes."

"I want to hire you."

Oh, please. Had it come to this? Did he want me to entertain for his daughter's birthday party?

The newspaper picture was over five years old. I noted that my face (hell, my whole body) was thinner then. The only thing thinner about me now was my hair. I no longer wore it in a pompadour, but combed it sideways to camouflage the V shape my hairline now insisted on.

I knew only too well the news article beside the photo. It

had been carried over UPI. Even though the article depicted me as a clever hero, a debunker of modern myths, the publicity had resulted in the indefinite shelving of my first network special. I never appeared on national TV again. The welcome mat for talk and variety shows was suddenly pulled in. The word was out: Colderwood was poison. Blackball him.

I might have understood the furor had it resulted from an eccentric political stance I had taken. Or if there had been a sex scandal—if there really are any sexually scandalous things left to do anymore.

I had done what any self-respecting magician would have. Harry Houdini did it. So did Dunninger. The Amazing Randi and Milbourne Christopher have built reputations on it. I did it, too.

Whenever I see the public taken in by a charlatan claiming psychic powers, I scream fraud as loud and as long as it takes to discredit him thoroughly. It never hurt my career before.

When I was a regular guest on the Griffin show, I debated so-called clairvoyants who claimed to aid police with tough cases. Sometimes I locked horns with astrologers who had grown fat from giving Hollywood stars precisely the advice they wanted to hear. Countless times I sat on the couch beside Johnny's desk, exposing the various ways the charlatan from Scotland bent metal objects with mediocre ocre sleight-of-hand methods rather than with "mind power."

It is easy now to look back and see where I should have drawn the line, when I should have kept my big mouth shut. My network special had been taped and edited. I was awaiting a time slot assignment. Weeks passed without any word.

One night I got a phone call from a woman who identified herself as a network secretary. She was so mealy-mouthed, I expected her to lose her nerve and hang up at any second. I gently coaxed her until I got the whole story.

From the time she hung up until I checked out all the facts and went public with the story, my rage was uncontrolled. Nothing could have stopped me.

What the informant told me was that the network programming executives had all but ceased relying on their high-paid analysts with their scientific methods. Instead, they were bankrolling a four-hundred-pound man from New Orleans who used a crystal ball. A direct phone line linked this man's living room to the office of the network entertainment director. The network was acting on more than 80 percent of this psychic's suggestions on which programs to cancel or renew. My network special was one of the casualties of his crystal ball.

After my press conference blew the lid off the scandal, I thought it would be just a short time before the airing of my program. Wrong. There was a major bloodbath in the upper echelon of the network. The new cadre was dead set against using me in any way. I was poison. I had bitten the hand that once fed me, and they were not going to let me get close enough for another chomp. I was put out of business just as quickly as the fat man from New Orleans.

I did not plummet immediately into obscurity. Instead, I was dragged gracelessly, rung by rung, down the same success ladder that I had climbed with such *sang-froid* during my more youthful days.

How can you tell when you have sunk as low as you can go? I guess I'll know that I'm really residing in the pits if that author shows up to do a chapter on me in one of his *Whatever Happened to . . . ?* books.

I dunked my tea bag and studied the man across from me. "You're not a writer, are you? You don't write about has-beens, do you?"

"No. I am no writer. Like I said, I just want to hire you."

Whew.

"First of all, you'll have to talk to my agent," I said.

"I just talked to your agent. He said you don't *have* an agent."

"Tough to bullshit anyone anymore, isn't it?" I said.

"The market for the stuff has dried up considerably in the past couple of years. Some say Watergate was the turning point."

"I'd say Abscam was. I heard that Allen Funt wants to buy the Abscam tapes and syndicate them as a series. Tell me, Mr.—"

"Morrow. L. Dean Morrow."

"Mr. Morrow, what kind of show do you want?"

"I don't want a show, Mr. Colderwood. I want to hire your talent, but not your entertainment talent."

"Nobody seems interested in that lately."

22

He tapped his finger on the newspaper clipping. "It's the talents you displayed *here* that I want to hire."

"I see. You're interested in my flair for pigheadedness, impulsive behavior, and self-destruction."

Morrow refolded the clipping and slid it back inside his pocket.

"For a man whose prospects are so limited, you're certainly not too anxious to diversify yourself."

"For a man I've known for only a few minutes, Mr. Morrow, you are awfully close to earning a lapful of hot tea."

His grin was sardonic. "We're ready to talk business, aren't we? The article mentioned a ten-thousand-dollar offer to anyone demonstrating paranormal ability under scientifically controlled conditions. That offer still good?"

"Nah. The ten thousand's gone. I blew it on luxuries like food and shelter."

"Anyone come close to earning it?"

"Not within a mile. That money was as safe as gold in Fort Knox. Once you learn the basic techniques these frauds use, you rarely come across something new. Magicians are constantly inventing new methods to fool the public, but these psychic phonies have been using the same crap for the past hundred and fifty years."

"I take it you have no belief at all in the paranormal."

"Not a whit. If you could show me even a minor miracle right now that I couldn't demystify, I'd give you the ten grand on the spot. If I had it, that is. The best I can offer right now is a quarter-pound hamburger. Without the cheese."

"You don't believe in ghosts or contact with the dead?"

"Mr. Morrow, the man with the closest contact with the dead is the guy who mows the cemetery lawn."

"What would you say if I told you I was being bothered by ghosts?"

"I would say there are several possible explanations. First, to put it bluntly, you could be a nut. There is also a chance you are gravely misinterpreting a phenomenon that is normal and natural. Also, someone could be playing a nasty trick on you. This someone might want to scare the hell out of you for reasons that only a psychiatrist could decipher.

"I could come up with a hundred perfectly earthly explanations for your ghosts. The last, the absolute last hypoth-

23

esis I would propose is that you are being haunted by genuine spirits from the Great Beyond."

"You think I'm crazy?"

"Maybe. Half the time I think *I'm* a ditso case. I'm no shrink. But you are right about my being qualified to find out who or what is causing your hobgoblins."

An ear-piercing beeping came from the rear of the restaurant. We both flinched. One of the waitresses turned off the alarm above the french fry machine.

"You said misinterpreting natural phenomena was also a possibility," he said.

"Sure. Here's a personal example. Both my parents grew up in a coal town in the western part of this state. Today it's a ghost town—no pun intended—with just a few crumbling foundations left. Even with a map, the site is difficult to find.

"My mother used to tell about an old black man that lived in the village. He was a barber who eked out an existence during the depression years. One night he was found dead in a wooded area near his house. His throat had been slit with his own razor. The murder was never solved.

"Not long after his death, the local folks reported hearing his ghost. Even my mother claimed to have heard him. Near the murder scene, she said, she plainly heard the old barber's voice repeatedly ask, 'How about a shave? Want a shave?'

"I loved to hear that story. A few years ago, I decided to look for an explanation. I interviewed my mother for hours, drawing out all the details I could. I even got her to draw a map of the area. I postponed a national tour of a full-evening magic show just so I could devote a month of research to the story of the murdered barber. I logged well over a hundred interviews with former residents of the town and some of their descendants. I practically lived in the morgue rooms of three different newspapers and in the reference sections of two libraries. To culminate my investigation, I spent three days camped out within thirty feet of what I believed to be the murder scene."

I finished off the last of my hamburger and dabbed my face with a napkin. Morrow hung on my every word. I love audiences. Even when they consist of only one person.

"The first night I didn't hear anything, and I damn near caught pneumonia. But the next two nights, I actually

24

heard the guy, as clearly as you hear my voice now. His vocabulary was very limited, though. The only thing he could say was, 'Have a shave?' Over and over.

"After a little poking around in the daylight, I found that the ghostly words were being emitted from a certain tree. That's right. A tree. When the wind blew from one direction, with a certain intensity, the branches rubbed together and produced the sound.

"I can't say it was the same tree that made the sound all those years ago. Perhaps that kind of tree always emits that kind of noise in the wind. What I do know is that my mind supplied rational meaning to perfectly natural sounds. When I played a tape recording of the tree creakings for people who didn't know the ghost story, they couldn't hear any words. But if I first told people about the barber with the slashed throat and said that I had miraculously captured the sound of his poor spirit moaning on tape, they were able to detect the ghost's eerie words."

"You didn't solve the murder case, then?"

"That wasn't my intent. For all I know, the murderer could have been one of the residents I interviewed. Boy, wouldn't that make you nervous, to have committed a crime all those years ago and then have some guy pop up decades later with lots of questions?"

Morrow nodded. "I don't think my ghosts are a result of natural causes, as you would put it."

"Mr. Morrow, can I then assume you believe that residents of the hereafter have the talent, or even the interest, to seek a return engagement in this world?"

"No. Not really," he said, with only slight hesitation.

"Congratulations. Welcome to the ever-decreasing ranks of the sane and the rational."

"That leaves us, then, with only one explanation."

"Yes," I said. "Someone is playing some very vicious games with your head."

"Will you help me find out who it is?"

"Nope. I'm an entertainer, not a hired snoop."

"Correction. You are an *unemployed* entertainer. And most likely flat broke."

"But not for long," I said, standing up. "If you'll excuse me, I've got some phone calls to make. Collect, of course. Before the evening is over, I'll have some kind of tempo-

25

rary work lined up, even if it's lecturing at a magicians' convention."

Without a word, Morrow hoisted a stack of bills from his pocket. They were all twenties. He started counting them. In a few seconds there was enough money on the table to pay the motel bill that I intended to welch on. In another couple of seconds there was enough money to keep me eating for at least three more weeks.

"Tell me when to stop. You realize this is just a down payment. You'll get the rest when you get results."

"Put that money away. Remember where you are. Those kids out in the arcade would string up their own moms for that kind of money. There's enough there to play Donkey Kong for a week and still have enough left over for acne medicine."

"I don't expect a lot for my down payment, only that you listen to my story and tell me what you think. If you are willing to help me out, I'll pay more. Five thousand dollars all told, whether you are successful or not."

I drained the rest of my tea, trying to think of a reason not to get involved with Morrow and his ghosts. I couldn't.

I squared up the pile of money and slipped it into the side pocket of my tux coat. I promised myself that I would listen to his story but then find a gracious way to beg off, keeping his down payment, of course. His poltergeists were probably caused by nothing more than a leaky faucet or a drafty house.

"I feel like a politician right now," I said, patting my pocketful of money. "I'll get us something to drink, and you can narrate this true-life campfire story of yours."

"No. Not now." He took a fresh napkin and wrote on it with a pen. He slid it across to me.

"Meet me there at eleven o'clock tomorrow night," he said.

"Is this your home?"

"No. It's just a street corner."

"You won't tell me your story now, but you will tomorrow night on a cold street corner. Maybe I was wrong. Maybe you are screwed up."

Sane or insane, he was not getting his money back.

"I can't talk anymore now. Be there tomorrow night. I guarantee you'll understand why it has to be this way. It was nice doing business with you, Mr. Colderwood," he said, picking up his coat.

He inched his way out of the booth. "Just don't be surprised at *anything* tomorrow night," he said.

After Morrow left, I felt a familiar flutter. Stage fright. I usually experienced it only a few minutes before a show. But the butterflies, or whatever insects were supposed to be in there, were really churning up a storm now.

I looked down at the napkin. Beside the drawing of the little man with the big hamburger head were the words "5th St. and 14th Ave." The least I could do before tomorrow night was to find out just who L. Dean Morrow was and what was located at the intersection of Fifth and Fourteenth.

Morrow's money was burning a hole in my pocket. First things first. I was going to buy a pack of cigarettes. My current pack was flattened, containing one last, lonely, very crooked butt. I straightened and smoothed it. It was still crooked. I decided to smoke it anyway. For symbolic reasons.

As I left the restaurant, the FM radio was emitting a rendition of "Johnny B. Goode." The orchestra, with its lush string section, didn't play it the way Chuck Berry probably likes it played. But then, Chuck Berry probably doesn't play it the way he used to, either.

I lit up my Camel. It was half smoked before I tasted any of it.

CHAPTER THREE

The last time I had ridden in a police car was when I was seven years old and had run away from home. The cops picked me up six blocks from my house. They both laughed when I asked if I had reached California yet. On the way back home they let me ride up front and talk into their radio. One of them even let me wear his hat.

I did not think any of the officers would go for that kind of fun tonight. I sat in the back with the one called Sarge. His real name was Paul Fetterman. I had demanded to see his ID, and he had obliged without comment. He was saving all his talk for downtown.

Downtown was, literally, downtown. At least what remained of it. Nearly half the stores were vacant, with windows soaped over or displaying signs that read, "For Rent. Fine Business Opportunity."

The Bayorvale City Hall was a solemn, three-story brick structure that stood beside a McDonald's. I wondered if Fetterman and his police buddies ate there.

Mounted atop the City Hall was a miniature Eiffel Tower radio antenna. All the building's windows were clear glass except for a section of translucent ones on the third floor. I figured that to be where the lockup is.

A modest yellow and black sign at the entrance proclaimed that the building also doubled as a fallout shelter. How comforting. Above the entrance was a ten-foot string of Roman numerals. They whisked me underneath them so quickly I couldn't calculate just how old City Hall is.

After a hiccuping elevator ride and a long walk through a corridor maze, we entered a room that could have doubled as my Sunday-school room when I was eight. It had the same long table with folding legs, the same gray metal

28

folding chairs, and the same stark yellow walls. Only the Sunday-school room didn't come equipped with a stenographer ready to record my every word.

Fetterman read me my rights and asked if I understood them. He handed me a paper, which contained the same words. He instructed me to read them, then asked if I understood. Finally, he had me sign the paper. I felt as if I was applying for a loan.

"Am I under arrest?"

"No."

"Then why the business with the rights?"

"Bitter experience, Mr. Colderwood. A good cop needs to be more like a magician every year to ensure that evidence he knows is good will be admissible in court. I take no chances. Some days I want to read the Miranda to the checkout girl just to make sure I get my groceries."

The stenographer's fingers fluttered over her machine. Fetterman's interest in the Constitution seemed reborn now that everything was being recorded.

"Mr. Colderwood, did you know a man by the name of L. Dean Morrow?"

"No." Lie Number One. The Big One. I decided to seize the ball and run as long and hard as I could. If I denied everything, I just might string together enough lies to get me out of this room and out of this town. The unvarnished truth would lead to too many questions. Particularly the part about the ghosts.

"What were you doing at the corner of Fifth Street and Fourteenth Avenue at eleven tonight?"

"I told you. Jogging."

"For twenty minutes on the same corner?"

"Sometimes I like to jog in place."

"Kind of a funny habit for a jogger, isn't it? I mean, those cigarettes?"

"You didn't give up sex when you found out about herpes and gonorrhea, did you?"

"No, but it certainly instilled in me a lot more caution when it came to participating in that form of physical fitness."

"To some people, caution is just another nuisance that hinders the enjoyment of life," I said.

The corners of Fetterman's mouth flickered, but he succeeded in suppressing the grin. He picked up a yellow envelope, pulled out an eight-by-ten glossy, and dropped it on the table in front of me.

"But some people never enjoy life," he said. "In fact, some hate life so much, they can't stand to see someone else enjoying it. A few get so pissed off, they even kill over it."

The photograph was definitely not taken in any studio. No fog filters or airbrushing. The details were sharp and clear. It showed a corpse, face down, on a sidewalk. I did my best to feign nonreaction, but I was not as practiced at the art as the steno. A robot with nimble fingers, she kept recording without a pause.

"Morrow?" I said.

"What was left of him. I'm sorry. You'll have to put that away. No smoking in this room."

I took the cigarette from my lips and slid it back into the pack.

Fetterman sat on the edge of the table. I had to tilt my head back to look him in the eye.

Two springy tufts of hair drooped down over his forehead on either side of the widow's peak. They bobbed when he moved, and he did not bother to brush them back.

"Pretty package, isn't it? Morrow plunges to his death from atop our city's one and only parking garage. The coroner sees nothing about the circumstances of death that point to anything other than suicide. We talk to his wife and business associate, and they say Morrow was acting depressed and despondent lately. There is no suicide note, but, statistically, suicide victims leave notes only about one-third of the time. A very neat package. This case is just begging for all the right rubber stamps and signatures so it can be filed away and forgotten. A textbook case. And, speaking of textbooks—"

He reached into the envelope and pulled out a single sheet of paper. He put it in front of me. I was grateful that it covered up the picture of Morrow's corpse.

"Read it," he said. "I'll wait until you're done. I got the time. And I won't tell anyone if you move your lips."

The paper was a photocopied page from a book titled, simply, *Homicide*. It took me less than a minute to read.

"Done already. You're fast."

"Where's the next page?" The paper he had shown me contained a summary of the facts of a case but did not give

30

any of the investigators' conclusions. The case involved a Cleveland woman whose body was found eight feet away from her apartment building, apparently crushed from a fall from an upper floor. Her husband reported to police that she had tripped and fallen off the balcony.

"The next page, the solution, is still in the envelope here," Fetterman said. "But I'm interested in your analysis. You've got all the facts you need right in front of you."

"How long ago did this happen?"

"Forty years. But that's beside the point. I want you to see what we policemen are sometimes up against. You've got all the facts laid out in black and white. You don't even have to dig. If you were the officer in charge, what would your conclusion be? Suicide or foul play?"

He clearly wanted me to either say suicide right away, or else sit there and gnash my teeth in indecision. I did neither.

"It was murder for sure, Sergeant. I think the lady's husband got a little too pushy."

His eyebrows sprang upward with surprise.

"Oh, yeah? What makes you so goddam sure?"

"Earlier tonight, when you told me about Morrow smacking into the pavement, you asked me if I had taken physics. That same physics class tells me that it's impossible for this lady's body to have landed eight feet away from the building—if she had fallen *or* jumped—no matter how far a drop it was. If she couldn't jump eight feet while standing on firm earth, she could not spring out far enough from the building to land eight feet away from it. Someone pushed her. Hard. According to your data here, the only one home was her husband. He did it. If he hadn't been so consumed with zeal when he gave her the final send-off, no one would have known. Had a running start, didn't he?"

"You're the first person I've ever known that got it right on the first try."

"What I do for a living is more or less a distant cousin of this sort of thing. Instead of trying to solve puzzles, though, we magicians work backwards. We create them."

He took the paper out of my hand.

"How far away from the building did Morrow land?" I asked.

"Close enough to have jumped all by himself." He put the paper back into the envelope. If there were more brainteasers from the annals of criminology in the envelope, he decided to leave them be.

"Morrow's death reminds me of the case I just showed you. Everything looks good, but nothing smells right."

"Why don't you show me the results of your preliminary investigation," I said. "Maybe I can give you some ideas. Fresh input."

"Colderwood, you're not looking at the file. You're *in* it. Among Morrow's personal effects was a slip of paper, folded tight, that had 'Fifth and Fourteenth, Sunday, eleven P.M.' written on it. We interpreted the numbers as a street and avenue, but we didn't know which was which. So we staked out Fifth Avenue and Fourteenth Street, too. The men there didn't see anything unusual. They did make a juvenile arrest—two kids vandalizing a neighbor's porch with raw eggs. But at the other intersection we found you. And you, Colderwood, do not make any sense at all. How about telling us where you fit in?"

I was glad that I had thrown out the smiling hamburger napkin with Morrow's handwriting on it.

"Where were you at one o'clock this morning, Colderwood?"

"With two old friends. Merv Griffin and David Letterman. The TV reception's really awful at the motel, let me tell you."

"TV's no alibi. I suppose you could tell us in detail what you watched, but it wouldn't prove anything. They were probably reruns. There are more reruns than new shows these days."

He took a pipe and tobacco pouch from his jacket pocket and began to fill the bowl.

"I thought you said no smoking."

"That's right. I did." He took out a pipe tool and tamped down the tobacco. "You didn't know about Morrow's death?"

"I told you, I never heard of Morrow before tonight."

"You didn't read in the paper or hear on the radio about a guy jumping off a building?"

"No. I don't have a radio. And today's Sunday. If I were going to buy a newspaper—and I rarely do—it would definitely not be on Sunday. The last paper I read was over a week old. There was a real uplifting article about the high rate of accident victims being robbed by ambulance attendants. I consider newspapers to be a highly dangerous, habit-forming drug of the depressant variety."

Fetterman fired up his pipe. The tobacco smelled like a mixture of spearmint and stale fruit.

"I have a reputation in this department, Colderwood, and it's mostly a bad one. I don't give up on anything. The men below me hate my guts because I push them too hard. My superiors hate me because I'm not afraid to rock the boat. On the occasions where I manage to perform outstandingly, their goodwill lasts exactly five minutes. I've been fired and rehired four times. I am hell on bookkeeping. There is one case I've been working on for fourteen years: a missing six-year-old girl. Her parents are the only ones who appreciate my perseverance. Every couple of months, the chief calls me into his office and orders me to drop the investigation. I always promise to stop, but I never do."

He made rapid smacking noises with his lips in an attempt to keep his pipe lit.

"I don't know how you're mixed up in all this, Colderwood, but when I find out, I'm going to tack your ass to the department bulletin board as my own personal trophy."

I glanced at the stenographer and saw that her fingers were resting at ease. I had not seen Fetterman give her a signal, but she had omitted his last statement from the record. I wondered how much she charged for an eighteen-and-a-half-minute gap.

Fetterman handed me a calling card with his name and two phone numbers on it. "Give me a ring in case your memory or your conscience straightens out."

I pocketed the card. At least it was one step above a hamburger napkin. "You're never going to drum up any business with cheap cards like this, Sergeant. You should consider investing in a nice art cut on a buff-colored card. After that you can move up to a three-color brochure and a direct mail campaign."

"I'm not in the entertainment business, and frankly, after our little conversation, I don't see how you're making any money at it either."

"Funny you should bring up the subject. I am, shall we say, at a crossroads in my career. I don't know where I'll be working next. But as soon as I line up something, I'm taking permanent leave of this town. If you call my motel

33

room after tomorrow, you'll most likely be talking to two high school kids skipping class to indulge in a quickie, or whoever else has the lapse in taste to rent a room like that. Just don't think I'm leaving town for any other reason than to make money."

Fetterman nodded, but was clearly unconvinced. He held the door for me, but I waited for him to leave first. I was not sure I could find my way out of the labyrinth of hallways. Maybe he had wanted me to go first because it was some sort of secret intelligence test. The first stoolie to wander out of the maze and make it to the pound of cheese on the captain's desk gets the C-note.

As we wended our way out, he informed me that I would have to provide my own transportation back to the motel. I reminded him that I did not have cab fare. He told me that I could make it on foot.

"Only three miles. You're a jogger. I know you are. You told me."

I opted for the stairs rather than the ancient elevator. Even though I was wearing a pair of Adidases, my footsteps still echoed. I heard faint bellows of laughter coming from the upper floor, where I had left Fetterman to shoot the breeze with two other detectives.

I had told the truth about leaving town tomorrow. I was only mildly curious about the circumstances surrounding the demise of L. Dean Morrow. I was right the first time when I told Morrow that his ghosts were all in his head. If he had wanted to line my pockets with a few hundred bucks before he and his ghosts stepped off the side of a building, more power to him.

If I had told Fetterman about Morrow's delusions, it would have given more support to the theory that his death was a suicide. But I had fibbed rather early on in the interview, so changing my story would have just heightened his suspicions.

"Mr. Colderwood. Mr. Colderwood. Could you wait up?"

I tried to outdo the pace of the footsteps I heard above me, but my pursuer must have been in better shape than I. He caught up with me just before I reached the ground floor.

"Mr. Colderwood, I—"

He took a few seconds to get his breath while I tried to pretend that I did not have to. He was a short, elfin man.

His long nose and chin accentuated the pointiness of his ears. He was bald, and his short hair on the sides did little to downplay his prominent ears. He wore a yellow turtleneck shirt and carried a tan jacket in one hand and a fur-lined hat in the other.

"You guys decide to book me or something?"

"I'm not a cop." His voice was deep and resonant, the kind that could sell beer, power tools, and sports cars on Sunday afternoon TV. I recognized him as one of the men standing around the coffee maker upstairs in the squad room.

"I heard you need a lift back to your motel. I thought I could help you out."

"Okay by me, if it doesn't cost too much."

"Don't worry. It's free."

"Nothing's free."

"You're right. That's what I keep telling my patients. I'll level with you. All I want is to talk with you awhile."

"Patients? You a doctor?"

"A psychiatrist."

"Fetterman acts fast, doesn't he? You supposed to check me out? To take an inventory of my marbles or something?"

"No, I have no connection whatsoever with them upstairs. I'm just a visitor, like yourself. It's a personal aim of mine to talk with as many different kinds of people as I can. I've never met a professional magician before."

"Then we're even. I've never met a professional psychiatrist. Only amateurs. That's not to say I've never had the urge to talk to one of your kind before. But I never got any further than consulting the Yellow Pages. By that time, things always seemed to iron themselves out."

"How about a beer, or maybe something stronger?"

"You'll have to buy."

"Sure. Just remember. Nothing's free."

"Don't worry. If it's war stories you're after, I'm loaded with them. Some are even true."

I slipped on my wool watch cap, and he put on his hat. It was as furry as a small cat. A lone feather grew out of its band.

"I never could understand why people wear hats like that," I said. "You look like a Bavarian whoremaster."

"When you have as little hair left as me, you care more

about staying warm than about flattening out your thirty-dollar hairstyle. Hey, you don't have much room to talk. That hat of yours makes you look like a Canadian Jack La Lanne."

"What bar's going to let us in dressed like this?"

"You kidding? The bar I go to will give us the best stools in the house. How come I have to pay for everything, anyway? I remember reading where you were supposed to have a million-dollar TV contract."

"I'll tell you about that exploit over the beer. Why are you bitching about spending a few bucks? I thought psychiatrists had Brinks trucks to haul their money to the banks. I even heard that you guys were the first ones in the medical profession to give up house calls. Real trendsetters."

"Oh, on occasion we still make house calls," he said as we approached the double glass doors of the lobby. "Sometimes we even get there before people jump off buildings. And sometimes we don't."

So he *did* expect more than just amusing stories for his investment. He was involved somehow in the Morrow case.

Nothing is free.

CHAPTER FOUR

Only when you attempt something requiring a modicum of coordination do you realize just how much you have had to drink. The phone inside my motel room kept ringing, and I, the winner of six first-place trophies in sleight of hand at international magicians' conventions, failed miserably at putting together all the skills necessary to get my damn door unlocked.

I turned and gave Dr. Randy Pescatore a go-ahead wave. The psychiatrist lightly bipped his horn and cautiously steered his Audi out of the parking lot.

I returned to the task at hand and triumphantly got the door open. When I picked up the phone, I could not hear anything, not even a dial tone. I then noticed that my wool hat was covering my ears. I took my hat off, but got only an earful of dial tone. Too late. I couldn't think of anyone who would call me at this hour, and I couldn't think of anyone I wanted to talk to.

I flopped facedown on the bed. Randy Pescatore had been right about the bar. The crowd there was rough and loud. The only times the jukebox was audible were the two times the place cleared out to watch street fights. Dr. Randy and I were the best dressed in the house. No one made fun of the way we were dressed, but someone did steal the good doctor's Bavarian whoremaster hat a half hour after we got there.

He reassured me that the place was not as tough as it looked. In addition to his private practice, he worked several hours a week for the mental health wing of Bayorvale Hospital. Many of his clients frequented the bar. To gain insight into the varied places where people seek solace, Pescatore began visiting Dick and Fred's Tavern. He took a liking to it and soon became a regular. He was on speaking terms with half the patrons. It was the other half that worried me. Particularly whoever stole his fur hat.

Neither of us could get the other drunk enough to reveal why he was really at City Hall tonight. I clung to my story about being in the wrong place at the wrong time, and he kept insisting that it was his professional interest in suicide and in the training of crisis-intervention specialists. He also insisted he knew nothing more about L. Dean Morrow than that the man ran a bookstore in town.

Pescatore was a skilled questioner. He would change the subject and, after I downed another beer or two, would try to catch me off guard by firing an innocent query about Morrow's death. Alcohol did not impair his psychiatric skills, although his questions did become considerably less succinct as the night wore on. He was superb at drawing the factual and emotional truth from me. That's his profession. But I was equally good at masking and coloring the truth. That's my profession.

We arrived at a tacit truce and decided to call it a night at about two in the morning, shortly after Pescatore told me the story behind the name of Dick and Fred's Tavern. Fred was the present owner. Dick was dead. About five years earlier, Fred had put a big hole in Dick's chest with a big gun. The death was ruled a justifiable homicide. Self-defense. It was then that I demanded to leave ——— and Fred's and go back to the motel.

Now the phone in my room started up again. This time I picked it up on the first ring. But the handset, much like my room key, became slippery and fell to the floor. By the time I picked it up again, the man at the other end of the line was saying, "Hello. Hello."

"Yeah?"

"Colderwood?"

"Yeah."

"I was getting tired of calling. I didn't think you were ever getting back."

"Who is this?"

"Listen close. I'll say this only once."

"What?"

"Listen close. I'll say this only once."

"Well make up your mind. Want me to get a pencil?"

"Just listen. Your presence in Bayorvale is not wanted."

38

"Believe me. The presence of Bayorvale in my life is not particularly wanted, either. Sir, our connection is really poor. Your voice sounds funny. Almost like you've got a handkerchief over the mouthpiece. Mind if I call you back? What's your number there?"

"You on drugs or something? If you don't butt out of this Morrow thing, bad things are going to happen to you."

"Such as?"

He proceeded to outline my possible physical fate. His gruesome account was so thorough and detailed, I thought he might be referring to prepared notes.

"Sir, I believe that you would have made your point by chopping off my arms. Running over me with a pickup would be redundant. But I will heed your warning. I'll leave town tomorrow."

"You will?"

He sounded surprised. I must have deviated from the script of his threatening call.

"Well, uh. Have a safe trip, you hear?" After a long pause, he said, "You sound drunk. Are you going to remember all this?"

"Sure. Right now I'm just trying to decide if I should return the key to the city to the mayor in person, or if I should just ship it back UPS."

He hung up.

I noticed an envelope on the floor in front of the door. I had missed it when I stumbled in. Inside was a note from the night clerk. I was supposed to call the number written at the end of the note. Was the threatening caller dumb enough to leave his number?

After the first ring, a man answered.

"Hello. This is L. Dean Morrow speaking."

CHAPTER FIVE

In a few seconds I realized the voice of L. Dean Morrow was a recording. After his brief introduction, Morrow was kind enough to give me a chance to leave a message on his machine. Since I had such a reputation for refuting arguments that the dead could contact the living, I was not about to begin acting as if the opposite were possible. I hung up.

I set my alarm for 5:00 A.M. I knew for sure I could contact Michael Horne at that hour. He specialized in closeup magic at New York City nightclubs and after-hours clubs. At 5:00 he would be just getting in from a night's work. I hoped he would let me stay at his apartment for a few weeks until I lined up another paying endeavor.

I momentarily considered calling my agent, Marlon Tate, and repeating some of the more violent details of the threatening call I had gotten. That crank call had stimulated my imagination.

My head sank into my pillow, and it seemed about two seconds had elapsed before the alarm clock buzzed me awake again. After a groggy-voiced Horne consented to my crashing at his apartment, I pulled the clock plug out of the wall and began to sleep in earnest.

Runner's high is a lie. I do not care how many starved-looking people on television tout the euphoric effects of jogging. It is all bunk.

When I woke up on Monday, the afternoon was well under way. My mouth tasted as if I had eaten too much of the wrong thing and not drunk enough of the right thing. My distorted logic told me that if I pulled on a sweat shirt and a pair of running shorts and pranced around for a couple of miles in the November chill, I would feel like a new man.

I ended up feeling like a new man, all right. My newness consisted of increased nausea, increased fatigue, and an increased desire for nicotine. Theoretically, aerobic exercise releases a whole bunch of hormones called endorphins. They are supposed to be two hundred times as powerful as morphine, thus accounting for the increased feeling of well-being in runners and people who dance in tights to disco music. All my endorphins must have had a bad night, too. They never showed up. They were probably hiding out in the sleep section of my brain in their little endorphin beds with the covers pulled up over their heads.

Back in my room, I called the local bus station and learned that the next bus for New York City would not leave until tomorrow morning. I switched on the television and pulled a pack of poker-size Aviator playing cards and a pack of regular-size Camels out of my suitcase. I immediately recognized the installment of "The Merv Griffin Show" as being the same one that was aired the night before last, when Morrow took his dive off the building. Fetterman was right when he said that half of TV was reruns. I wondered if they still reran any of the Merv shows that I was on. Probably not. Too long ago.

I zipped through my complete regimen of sleights and flourishes with the deck of cards. I never tired of practicing the same series of steals, palms, false cuts, false shuffles, false counts, invisible cuts, bottom deals, and second deals. I had learned the moves when I was eight, and I don't recall a day since that I did not practice them. Even when I was in that Chicago hospital after swallowing too much water in an attempt to duplicate Houdini's Water Torture Escape, I demanded that someone run down to the gift shop and buy some cards. I cannot recollect the last time I used any of these so-called basic sleights in a paid performance. Many of them are arcane and, although reprinted in book after book, have little practical use. Yet I doggedly cling to my daily ritual. I get a pleasant glow after completing all the moves flawlessly. Who knows? Maybe the practice releases a few of those elusive endorphins.

When I finished, I put the cards back in their box. I removed one of the casters from the bed frame and made sure the money Morrow had given me was still there, stuffed up in the hollow space above the wheel. I considered the money a loan for the time being. When I got on my feet again, I would send an anonymous note of thanks and a money order to Morrow's widow.

I walked to the motel office and bought a copy of the *Bayorvale Dispatch.* Morrow's obituary was brief, explaining that more details would be included in a later edition. The article did not tell me anything I had not learned from a few phone calls after our meeting on Saturday. Morrow owned a bookstore called Editions. He was a member of the Bayorvale Kiwanis and the Sutter Avenue United Methodist Church. He was survived by his wife, the former Wanda Jeffreys. No children. The paper said he expired at 1:10 A.M. Sunday, "unexpectedly." Quite. Funeral arrangements were not yet complete.

I sat on the edge of my unmade bed and again dialed the number that the night clerk had written in his message. It rang eight times before someone answered. This time it was not a recording. It was a woman, and she spoke so softly I had to press the receiver tight against my ear to understand her. I introduced myself and explained that I was returning a call from the night before.

"This is Wanda Morrow," she said. "Did you try to call last night?"

"Yes, but I got the recorded message. I thought it was a joke and hung up. I almost didn't bother calling you today."

"When I went to bed, I turned on the answering machine. I really needed the sleep, but I didn't want to take the phone off the hook. Dean taught me how to turn the machine on and off, but never how to record a new message. I was hoping that if you called, you would leave a message."

Her speech was slurred, and I wondered if her sleep last night had been drug-induced.

"I would like very much to meet with you, Mr. Colderwood."

"I'm afraid that's impossible, Mrs. Morrow. I'll be leaving town very shortly. How did you get my name?"

"From Sergeant Fetterman. He told me which motel you're at."

42

"Then he probably told you that he questioned me last night."

"Yes, he called me late last night to give me an update on his investigation. Today he phoned to say that the county coroner had officially declared the cause of my husband's death as suicide. The coroner sees no reason to conduct an inquest."

I wondered if she could hear over the phone that my breathing had measurably relaxed.

"But the sergeant reassured me that he was not dropping his interest in this case. He's just going to be more discreet."

"Mrs. Morrow, I do not know what Fetterman told you, but let me assure you that I had nothing to do with your husband's death."

"Even if Sergeant Fetterman hadn't brought up your name, I think I still would have contacted you. I saw the advertisements for your show in the paper. I've seen you on television several times. Although not lately."

"No. Not lately."

"There are some things I didn't tell Sergeant Fetterman. Things which I couldn't tell him."

That makes two of us, Mrs. Morrow.

"But I would not feel at all uncomfortable discussing these matters with you, Mr. Colderwood. Because of your background."

"Could you be more specific, Mrs. Morrow?"

"No, I'd prefer not to talk about it on the telephone. I can understand your reluctance to meet with me. Sergeant Fetterman is not a very congenial man, even to a grieving widow. There are two reasons I believe you will see me today. The first is that if you refuse, I am going to call the sergeant, and, even though it is not true, I shall tell him that you knew my husband and were involved in a business deal with him. That would probably be enough for him to detain you and question you at least once more, enough to postpone your plans for leaving town."

"Maybe." I knew damn well it would.

"And the second reason is that I have three thousand dollars in cash that I would like to give you in return for a few small favors."

The Morrows must love to pass out money.

43

After she hung up, I took a hurried shower and dressed, trying not to think about what I might be getting into. I could feel those endorphins pull the covers over their little heads again, and I was certain it would be a while before they ventured out again.

CHAPTER SIX

It was a twenty-minute taxi ride from the motel to the Morrow home. After the driver discovered that I knew nothing about the Pittsburgh Steelers or even football in general, he contented himself to drive in silence. He did not even beep his horn. The cab was such a junker, maybe the horn was broken. A pair of jumper cables kept him company on the front seat. At every stop, he threw the transmission into park and gassed the engine to keep it from stalling.

I watched the scenery change from the close grouping of motels, discount stores, and fast-food restaurants to a long stretch of dilapidated houses that were well over eighty years old. The homes improved steadily, giving way finally to the exclusive Coronet Park section of town. None of the homes here looked older than two decades, and they were far enough apart so that you would have to shout to be heard by your neighbor.

When we pulled up in front of Morrow's, I was mildly surprised to find that although the house was as large and as opulent as its neighbors, it did not share their newness. Its stucco exterior had long since faded from white to pasty gray. Three stone arches, each wide enough to drive a car through, lined the front of the structure. Even though the nearest houses had kept their distance, the original owner had surely never envisioned the surrounding property being lined with streets and avenues. The neighborhood, with its one-story houses and two-car garages, clearly negated any stateliness the Morrow home once possessed.

I made a point of overtipping the driver, not knowing whether he would be the same cabby that would give me my return ride—if, indeed, Bayorvale had more than one cab. The sidewalk from the curb to the house was long enough for me to make the tough decision of which arch of the three I would walk through to get to the front door. To my left, bisecting the lawn, was a line of huge evergreen trees. They were so tall that the Morrows would have given up years ago worrying about some midnight thief sawing off one of them for personal use in his living room at Christmas time.

I chose the center arch. The enclosure formed by the arches was dark and musty. I glanced at my reflection in the dirty glass of the storm door. I was wearing no tie to straighten, but I did pull my sweater over so that the V would be centered with the buttons of my open-necked shirt. I wore a brown sports jacket with a gray tick pattern. I looked like a real estate salesman who was trying to blur the distinction between business and casual dress.

I pressed the doorbell button. The light above it was burned out. I did not hear a ding or a buzz or a chime. I tried again, holding it in longer. At last the front door opened. The woman and I stared at one another for a moment before I opened the storm door.

"I have an appointment to see Mrs. Morrow."

"I am Mrs. Morrow. Come in, Mr. Colderwood."

She was attractive in her plaid blouse and long, bright red skirt. She smiled graciously. There were no lines of grief or worry on her face. The only lines were ones you would expect on a woman in her early fifties. But that was exactly what I did not expect—a woman in her fifties. She was old enough to be Morrow's mother.

Her living room was full of things that were pretty to look at but never used. The mantelpiece around the fireplace was spotless and the fire irons were shiny.

On the mantel, two plates were proudly displayed. Their gingerbread design was so finely detailed that I would have had to move close to discern any of the individual lines. Beside the fireplace was a cream-colored wing chair with a matching ottoman. Both chair and ottoman were spotless.

On the coffee table, in front of the love seat where I sat, was a foot-high candle as big around as my arm. It had never been lit. Beside it was a covered candy dish and a volume of *Reader's Digest* condensed books. I was certain

46

that if I were to lift the cover of the candy dish, I would find it full.

Mrs. Morrow sat on the end of the couch, at right angles to the love seat. I turned down her offer of a drink or coffee.

"You do not look like a woman who gives in easily to the temptation of using blackmail. I want to leave this town. Very badly. I don't appreciate your trying to complicate my affairs."

"You do not look like the kind of man who gives in easily to the threat of blackmail."

"I'm here, aren't I?"

"Perhaps my mention of a few thousand dollars might have influenced your decision."

"Somewhat. But it wouldn't be the first time I chased after a dollar, only to discover that I didn't want it that badly. Just what is it you want?"

"I want you to find out why my husband is dead, Mr. Colderwood." Her eyes were moist, but with anger, not grief.

"Someone is already doing that. Sergeant Fetterman."

"No, he isn't. Sergeant Fetterman thinks he smells murder. If he can find someone to pin it on, it will simply be another milestone in his career. But if he changes his mind, decides that the whole incident was just a suicide, then he will drop his efforts immediately. He won't try to find out why Dean killed himself. That's why I need you. Murder or suicide, find out why my husband is dead."

"I am not a trained criminal investigator."

"You've solved cases before. What about that series of murders in—where was it?—Minnesota or North Dakota? I heard you talk about it on TV."

"You're referring to the Valentine's Day Murderer. That was in Minnesota. I didn't solve that case. That was the one where for five consecutive years a young girl was abducted and mutilated in a small community during the week of Valentine's Day. A psychic claimed that he could trace the killer. He turned up some astonishing items, including murder weapons and victims' wearing apparel."

"But you exposed the psychic as the real murderer."

"No. I simply proved conclusively to the police that he was a phony. They hired me to pose as a detective. I set up some tests that were strictly controlled by scientific methods. No self-proclaimed psychic or seer has ever passed one of my tests. When the police were convinced that the man

47

was a liar, they could only conclude that he either knew or *was* the actual killer. When the next February fourteenth rolled around, he fell right into the trap they set for him."

"But the psychology department at that university in Ohio certified him as being a genuine psychic."

"The head of that psychology department did not do his homework and devise tests not affected by the biases of the tester. No, I did not aid the police in solving the case. I simply caused them to take a fresh look at their supernatural stoolie."

"You have strong convictions about claims of the supernatural?"

"My convictions border on bigotry."

"Do you include ghosts on your list of nonbeliefs?"

It was turning into the same kind of conversation I had had with her husband.

"Mrs. Morrow, did Fetterman tell you why he picked me up?"

"Yes. Because of the note found in Dean's pocket. You refused to admit any connection with my husband. Sergeant Fetterman said you were lying."

I wanted a cigarette very badly, and I scanned the room for an ashtray or any kind of evidence that she smoked or did not mind her guests smoking. I did not see any.

I didn't feel like sitting anymore, so I walked over to the fireplace. I admired the decorative plates. Each had a bouquet of mostly red and blue flowers in the center. The rest of the design consisted of concentric circles of single flowers. Lying flat on the mantelpiece was a gold-framed photograph. She must have set it on its back so that she would not have to look at it. I picked it up.

"That picture was taken about five years ago."

The picture showed six couples and one man crowded around a table in a large restaurant or a ballroom. The tabletop was cluttered with glasses and women's purses. Everyone was laughing, probably at some stock joke the photographer had cracked so that the resulting picture would make everyone look as if they were having a jollier time than they really were.

"All those years Dean was in Kiwanis, and that's the only convention he made it to. That's him waving at the camera. The one wearing the tuxedo and the little black tie."

48

The burning inside me ignited and flared to full strength. I had felt glimmers of it when Fetterman questioned me, but I had been able to ignore it. But there would be no ignoring it from now on.

"You offered me three thousand dollars on the phone. I cannot promise you three thousand dollars' worth of results. And I certainly cannot promise that any answers I do produce are going to satisfy you."

I remembered the first time I experienced this inner burning. I was eight years old, and I had been invited onto our school stage to assist an assembly magician. I knew then that I would not be satisfied until I found out how he performed every bit of magic. It took me nearly a year. Books on sleight of hand were not as accessible as they are today. It was another year before I could perform the tricks as well as he did. It was still another before I began to win prizes and get my picture in magic magazines for the tricks I invented.

It was the kind of burning that made you forget when to eat and when to sleep. It could even make you forget that you wanted a cigarette.

"Mrs. Morrow, I can give you one week of my time. And no more. There are a lot of questions I must ask you first. All of them are personal."

She insisted on giving me the money now. "It'll take me a few minutes to get it. It's funny. I always chided Dean for keeping so much cash in the house."

She left the room, and I heard her walk up a flight of stairs.

I went over to a large window at one end of the living room. It was probably a picture window at one time. It was now divided by a wooden frame into smaller panes of glass. Each pane was latticed into diamonds. The window's light allowed me to examine the picture's details better.

No doubt remained in my mind. The man in the picture was not the man who had called himself L. Dean Morrow and presented me with an envelope of money two days ago. The man in the photo was at least twenty-five years too old.

CHAPTER SEVEN

I sat on the sofa beside Mrs. Morrow. I had tucked the envelope of money into my jacket pocket without counting it. On my lap was another photograph of L. Dean Morrow.

He had posed in front of the pine trees in his yard. His posture was stiff, and he clasped his hands unnaturally in front of him. He wore a dark blue suit and a white shirt. The blue tie had tiny white polka dots, and the knot was too big, causing the button-down collar of the shirt to flare out. Although his glasses were black horn-rims, the lenses were stylishly large. He was bald, and the gray hair on the sides of his head looked blue in the photo. Perhaps the camera shutter had captured his face while it was halfway toward forming a smile; his lips formed a straight line, yet his face expressed mild amusement.

"How old was your husband?" The obituary had mentioned no age.

"Forty-nine. Almost fifty."

"How long were you married?"

"Twenty-three years."

She told me they had lived in this house since their marriage. Her father had built the house, and she had grown up in it. Both of her parents were dead when she and Morrow had married.

Morrow had started his bookselling business shortly after their wedding. The shop never lost money, but had never shown more than a modest profit. Most of the business was mail order, although there were enough local customers to maintain a shop. Morrow loved books, but did not love business. He therefore delegated most of the day-to-day responsibilities to the manager of Editions, one Logan Zoller. The Morrows lived mostly on the money left to them by her parents.

"Most of my time is spent in this house. I don't belong to any clubs or organizations. I like interior decorating. It doesn't take me long to tire of the look of a room and decide that it must be done over. You know, I never even learned to drive. Guess I'll have to learn, now."

"Do you have any children?"

"None. We made that decision before we married. We never changed our minds, and we never quarreled over it."

"Was your marriage a happy one?"

"We got along, and we tried not to get in each other's way. Sure, there were arguments. He complained that the furniture and wall colors changed so often that he never felt entirely at home. And I would get grouchy when I thought he had his nose stuck in a book too much."

"No affairs?"

"None that he cared enough to tell me about. As for myself, the opportunity failed to present itself, even once. I doubt, though, that I could have gotten serious enough about someone to tell Dean about it."

I was prepared to ease off if I thought my questions were beginning to disturb her. Her voice had grown slightly tremulous, but she did not seem anywhere near tearfulness. So I pressed on.

"During the last week or so, was there any change in your husband's behavior?"

"I told Sergeant Fetterman that Dean had been acting despondent. That was an understatement. If I had told him the truth, he would have stopped his investigation and written my husband off as a mental case. In the two weeks preceding his death, he had trouble sleeping. When he did manage to doze off, he would wake up with a start. I didn't see him pick up a book in those last two weeks. He refused to confide in me.

"About a week ago, I awoke in the middle of the night. It was three A.M. Every lamp and light in the bedroom was on, and Dean was not in bed beside me. I walked as quietly as I could out into the hallway. I could see there was a light on downstairs. I heard talking. I thought we were being robbed, so my first impulse was to run back into the bedroom and get Dean's gun out of the nightstand. I sneaked halfway down the stairway. When you grow up in a house, you learn where to walk on each step so it doesn't creak. He was sitting right here on this sofa, muttering to himself. His face was wet with tears. They ran down his face and dripped off his chin. He made no attempt to wipe them away or stop them."

"Could you hear what he was saying?"

"No. He looked like a stranger in his own home. I had never seen him cry before. At first, I wanted to run down the stairs and throw my arms around him and ask him what was wrong."

"Did you?"

"No. More than anything in the world right now, I wish I had. I suppose we were both cowards. He was too afraid to tell me what was troubling him, and I was too afraid to ask. Back in the bedroom, I turned off all the lights. I tried to stay awake and wait for him to come back to bed, but I must have drifted off. When I woke up again and— Wait, I should tell you that I'm not sure if what I'm about to say is a dream or if it really happened. I just don't know."

"That's all right. Go ahead."

"A tapping at the window woke me up. Some . . . some *thing* was looking in the window at me. And grinning. I lost control of myself. I started screaming and couldn't stop."

"What did you see?"

"I'm not sure. I can't even say if it was a man or an animal. It reminded me of photographs I've seen of those horrible World War II death camps. I saw the face of a man who was hovering somewhere between life and death. The only difference between his face and that of a skeleton was a thin layer of almost transparent skin. It was the face of a man who had no business being happy. That's what made me scream: his wide, toothless grin."

"Your husband hear you scream?"

"Yes, but the face was gone by the time he got up to the bedroom. I told him it was just a bad dream. We held each other all night. But we didn't talk. Dammit. We didn't talk."

I scribbled on the notepad that was balanced on my lap, giving her a few moments to compose herself.

"Is there a tree or a trellis located outside your bedroom window? Anything that could be readily climbed?"

She nodded. "A tree."

I took a silk handkerchief from my jacket pocket. I snapped it in the air and crushed it in my hands to show it was unprepared. I folded it on my lap, then rested my hands on my thighs on either side of the hank.

"Mrs. Morrow, some people believe so much in the supernatural, they reject many natural elements of life. They interpret their slightest good fortune as intervention by the gods. In turn, they view negative occurrences as the work of the devil. Anything that cannot be fully explained is considered either a curse or a miracle. That's why the first conjurers in the world were very powerful. In the last couple of centuries the magician's power was gradually usurped by the scientist. There are still some individuals, though, who, in their quest for power and wealth, borrow from the crude fundamentals of our art and make claims of supernatural talents."

The hanky on my lap trembled and twitched.

"If you have the ability to frighten and deceive people, you indeed have a power to be reckoned with."

The silk bobbed up and down, each time rising a little higher. Something tangible underneath the handkerchief seemed to be garnering the strength to escape.

"Stories of ghosts and demons and extraterrestrials sell a lot of tabloids at supermarket checkouts."

The hank jerked madly up and down. It was on the verge of becoming airborne. My hands rested completely motionless on my lap. Mrs. Morrow timidly waved one hand in the air above the hunderkerchief, checking for threads. She found none.

"But ghosts don't exist, do they?" I whisked the silk off my lap, showed it on both sides, and crumpled it, showing that there was nothing inside it.

"Nifty trick, isn't it? Any eight-year-old with ten minutes of practice can perform it passably. Walk into any magic shop in the country, and you can buy this trick for four-fifty. As a matter of fact, a lot of eight-year-olds have scared the crap out of their parents with this beauty." I replaced the handkerchief in my pocket. "Mrs. Morrow, I'll try to get to the bottom of this for you."

I did not add that I also wanted to get to the bottom of who set me up. And why. I described for her the young man who had posed as her husband at the mall restaurant. She didn't know anyone who fit that description.

"Has your husband at any time sought psychiatric help?"

"No."

"Do you know who Randolph Pescatore is?"

"Yes, I do."

"How do you know him?"

"Oh, I don't really know him. I've seen his picture in the paper. Once they interviewed him on a local TV news series on rape. He gave a personality profile of the typical rapist."

"Did your husband have any enemies?"

"He had very few close friends. And no enemies that I know of."

"Know of anyone who might profit from his death?"

"No."

"Including you?"

"Including me. He did have some life insurance. I'm not sure it's still in force. It was taken out so long ago that inflation would surely have diminished its value by now."

"What about his partner?"

"Logan Zoller was not his partner, remember. He was a salaried employee. And now he'll be the sole owner of the shop. Dean left it to him in his will. But since the shop never did much better than cover its expenses, it won't be a gold mine for him."

"Did Mr. Morrow have any health problems?"

"Nothing serious. The family doctor constantly reprimanded him for not taking steps to lower his blood pressure, and he could have stood to lose some weight, but couldn't we all?"

I sucked in my stomach.

"You mentioned that he had a few close friends."

She gave me the name of the president of the local Kiwanis.

"And he had also struck up quite a relationship with a man named Homey."

"Homey. That's his first name?"

"I don't know. I never met him. Dean loved to play chess. When the weather was good, he would go to Webb Park, set up a board, and play with whoever showed up. The one he talked most about was an old man called Homey."

I wrote down the name, guessing at the spelling.

"Did you see the note that the police found on your husband? The one with the street corner written on it?"

"No. But Logan Zoller brought over the rest of Dean's personal effects. They're in the study. I haven't looked at them yet."

"Zoller brought them over? Why?"

"I refused to go downtown to identify the body, so Logan did that for me. The sergeant did coerce me into making a positive ID from some photographs. It was almost as bad. Concerning that note, though, Sergeant Fetterman said he wanted to hold on to it for a while."

"Did your husband act out of the ordinary on that last night?"

"Well, he didn't talk much. We both watched TV for a few hours. I fell asleep during the news. The phone call from the police station woke me up."

"You weren't awake when your husband left the house?"

"No. I have no idea why he went out."

"Can I take a look at your husband's personal effects?"

"Sure. Just follow me."

She led me down a narrow, carpeted hallway. Every door we passed was open wide, treating me to quick glimpses of soft colors and balanced placement of furniture. If my visit had been of a social nature, I am sure she would have given me a guided tour, filling me in on all the artistic and practical factors that influenced her decorating decisions.

The last doorway in the hall was closed. She opened it, saying, "This is his study. It was his refuge, where he went to be alone. You'll understand if I don't go in?"

"Sure. How about that cup of coffee you offered?"

She nodded and left me standing alone in the study doorway. Mrs. Morrow probably kept the door closed even when her husband was alive. The room was one hell of a mess. Even by my standards.

There was just enough space in the study for the desk, chair, and two bookcases. I flicked the light switch on the wall, but nothing happened. Either the bulb was burned out, or the switch was faulty. I tried the desk lamp. It worked, but illuminated the desk top and little else. The bulletin board hanging on the wall above the desk was warped and was probably purchased from a five-and-dime. It was plastered with bits of paper and clippings from booksellers' and publishers' magazines. Some papers were

55

taped right on the wall. The desk top was stained from wet rings left by cups and glasses. The only area that showed any degree of neatness was the bookshelves. Rows of books stood perfectly straight and appeared to receive regular dustings.

In the middle of the desk was what I was looking for: a clear plastic bag secured with a twist tie and police tag. I spread out the contents on the desk. The eyeglasses looked like the same ones Morrow wore in the picture in the living room. Both lenses were missing, and the frames were cracked. I thumbed through a black appointment book. Most of the pages were blank. There was no mention of a Sunday night appointment with me or anyone else. I lined up the rest of the contents of his pockets—a handful of change, a key ring loaded with new shiny keys, a half-consumed roll of Tums, a ball-point pen, a handkerchief, a wallet.

I opened up the wallet and flipped through the plastic picture holders and peeked inside all the little slots and leather enclosures. There were six ones in the billfold. All the major credit cards were stacked vertically, each one in its own leather slot. The photo section was filled with snapshots, except for one space. I poked my finger in the empty plastic pocket. It felt loose and pliable enough to have once contained a picture.

Mrs. Morrow returned with a silver tray containing a cup of coffee and a sugar bowl and creamer. She stood her ground in the doorway, still refusing to enter. I took the tray from her, put it on the desk, and sat back down in the office chair. She blocked what little outside light could seep into the tiny, windowless room. I turned the desk light to the high-intensity setting. That only served to focus a stronger spotlight onto the desk top, making the room even darker by comparison. Mrs. Morrow became a silhouette in the doorway. The lines and creases in her face were softened, and the gray in her hair was darkened. The change in lighting made her look twenty years younger and twenty years prettier. I felt very much the intruder.

I took a sip of the coffee. Unfortunately, like most coffee, it did not taste as good as it had smelled.

"I'm sorry that you had to bring the cream and sugar. I forgot to tell you that I take it black."

"I forgot to ask."

"Do you know any of these people?" I asked, opening up the photo section of Morrow's wallet.

"Let me look. I never went through his wallet before."

I returned to the doorway and handed her the wallet. She flipped through the plastic inserts, trying to conceal her shaking hands. I looked away, taking little swallows of the coffee.

"Most of these pictures are of me. The other people are relatives."

She handed the wallet back to me.

"You wouldn't mind if I went through his desk, would you?"

She shrugged and said it was all right.

"What do you think of my coffee?"

"I like it fine."

"It's a Viennese roast. Some people have told me it's too strong."

"It's fine."

"Would you like to take some with you?"

"What? Sure. Sure, I'd like that."

She turned and walked down the hall. Meanwhile, I foraged around in the private world of L. Dean Morrow.

The mess was a deception. There was not much in the desk to examine. If Morrow had ever taken time to straighten out its contents, he could have placed everything in one drawer. I found nothing of consequence, just casual correspondence with other booksellers, subscription notices from magazines, more clipped advertisements and articles, and a sizable collection of paper clips, rubber bands, and thumb tacks.

When Mrs. Morrow returned, she carried a white paper bag. It contained a tin of coffee beans. Did I imagine she was going to bring me a big Styrofoam cup with a plastic lid, like a take-out order? As we walked back to the living room, she gave me explicit instructions on how to brew the perfect cup of coffee.

I suspected that Morrow's little study was his statement against the cheerless elegance that dominated every cor-

57

ner of the home. I was sure that before long his gooseneck lamp, his stained and scarred desk, and the Woolworth's bulletin board would take up new residence at a Salvation Army showroom—and that Morrow's little refuge would thereupon become a walk-in closet.

Back in the living room, I telephoned for a taxi. Because of the heavy envelope of money, my coat hung down a little on one side. I could not find a way to adjust it so it felt comfortable.

"We had better have the same story to tell Sergeant Fetterman. He's not going to be thrilled about my sticking around Bayorvale. He's really going to be suspicious when I show up at the services for your husband."

"You needn't be concerned about the services. They won't be open to the public. Neither you nor the sergeant will be going. There will not even be a viewing. My husband's remains will be cremated, and our minister will conduct a short ceremony of remembrance here. It's what he wanted. Believe me."

"We'll still have to tell Fetterman something. If you were to review my personal finances, you would never know it, but I do have a bachelor's degree in business administration. Now, for perhaps the first time in my life, I am going to make use of my degree. If Fetterman asks, just tell him you are hiring me to assist in putting your personal and financial affairs in order."

She shook her head. "He won't buy it."

"Of course not. We both know that. But he would be disappointed if we didn't at least make an effort to lie."

She smiled and walked to the window. "Taxis always seem to take forever, don't they?"

The dimness of her husband's study had made her look younger. Now the light flooding through the window played no tricks. She looked not one day under fifty. But still very attractive. She turned slowly so I got a full view of her trim, full figure. Her smile was definitely one of invitation.

I remembered what she had said about the lack of opportunity when we had discussed extramarital affairs. I felt a mixture of pleasure and fear.

"It's a long way out to the street. I might not hear the horn," I said.

I assured her that I would keep her informed of any discoveries.

It was a relief to leave the Morrow house. I had never felt so closed in in such a large place. Waiting on the sidewalk for the taxi, I glanced back and saw Mrs. Morrow peering through the diamond design of the picture window. She looked like an inmate—inside a very elegant prison.

CHAPTER EIGHT

The cab that showed up was in better repair than the one I had taken earlier. I wish I could say the same about the driver—a different one, so I had overtipped in vain. The only tip I intended to give *this* guy would be to ease up on the chemical side of life. He talked incessantly, and his memory bank seemed blown out.

We cruised leisurely through the streets of Bayorvale while he recounted his life's story in absolutely no chronological order. I had told him to drive me to any car rental agency. After a half hour of meandering driving, he gave up. Now he was in a phone booth, flipping through the Yellow Pages, trying to find the address of a rental service. He could not remember the names of any of the local agencies. The names Avis or Hertz "possibly" rang a bell for him, but he was not sure of their locations. I suspected that the two-way radio in the cab was purely decorative, although I didn't rule out the possibility that the driver had forgotten how to work it.

"Okay, buddy. We're in business now," he said as he wedged himself behind the wheel again. He wore a white shirt with the sleeves rolled up. Sweat made his beard and the straight bangs on his forehead glisten. The November chill had me shivering, but this guy was complaining about the heat. Summer must really be a killer for him. Perhaps he switched pills when the seasons changed. We drove with the windows down.

"The door. Close the door before you start driving," I said, trying not to excite him.

"Oh. Yeah."

He pulled the door shut with such force, I thought he broke the glass inside it.

"Dale, before we log any more miles, could you tell me if you got the address of a car rental agency?"

"Jesus! You know my name. You a psychic or something?"

"No, Dale. Just the opposite. I know your name because your license is posted on the back of your seat."

"Oh. Yeah. I forgot."

"Dale, I have a hard time believing that you have a memory problem. Now, did you get an address?"

"Take your pick." He waved the Yellow Page that he had, literally, ripped off.

"Let me see," I said, scanning the page. "Low Rates Rental. Right up my alley. 1919 Thirty-second Avenue. Can you find that, Dale?"

"I'll sure give it a good fucking try, buddy."

"Great, Dale. Just keep your eyes on the road. I'll watch the streets and the numbers. You know, Dale, I guess I'm just not used to riding taxis in a small town. You left me sitting in your cab with the engine running for almost five minutes. I could have stolen your taxi and all your fares."

"Nah. I would have blown up the gas tank before you got one block." He turned halfway around in his seat, and he waved a gun in my face.

"Gawd! Put that thing away. Use both hands when you steer. Both hands."

The pistol was as big as a bazooka and heavy enough that it looked impossible to control using just one hand. He put it back down on the seat beside him.

"Turn left at the next intersection, Dale."

He turned right.

"Left. I told you left."

"I'm trying to shake our tail."

"Dale. Look in your rearview mirror. There's no tail behind us. Do you see anyone?"

"Not yet . . . wait, there it is, that blue Cougar."

"That Cougar is three cars behind us."

"Sure it is. That shows us we're dealing with a pro. Want me to shake him?"

"No. Don't even *think* about breaking the speed limit. Look, Dale, your mind's playing tricks on you."

He veered sharply into an alley. The tires made a mild protest. Sure enough, a few seconds later the Cougar followed suit.

61

"It looks more black than blue, Dale."

He cruised out of the alley and onto the next street. He pulled up on the sidewalk and executed a tight U-turn, reentering the street between a No Parking sign and a fire hydrant. Two women toting shopping bags dodged out of our way.

"Very fancy, but I can't see what all that accomplished," I said. "He's still following us. All he had to do was make a simple left."

Dale maintained his same slow speed until the light up ahead turned red. Then he floored it. I was propelled hard against the back seat, and I almost dropped Mrs. Morrow's paper bag of coffee. As he approached the intersection, Dale slammed on the brakes. The car fishtailed to a stop. He jerked into reverse and shot backwards a quick half block. He stopped the car, then veered sharply to the right. Our front tires bumped against the curb. We completely blocked the Cougar's path. I watched with detached fascination as the Cougar, its brakes fully applied, screamed toward us. It stopped six inches short of striking us broadside.

"Whew! Close business, eh, boss?" Dale said.

Horns behind the Cougar started to blast. People on the sidewalk stopped to watch. I reached inside my pocket and peeled a bill from the envelope.

"Take this, and thanks for nothing, Dale. Now, don't worry about me. I recognize the person in the Cougar now. I'm going to get out of the taxi and walk over to that car. As soon as you can, straighten out your cab and get moving down the street. I'll be all right. I don't imagine you have a permit to carry that cannon of yours, so please don't let anyone see it, okay?"

He took the money and nodded reluctantly.

As soon as I had jogged around the back of the cab, he pulled away, laying rubber the whole way up the block. The passenger side of the Cougar was unlocked. I jerked open the door and crawled in the front seat. The driver was blond.

"What's your name?" I asked.

She refused to answer and just drummed her fingers on the steering wheel. As I patiently waited for a response, the cars behind us picked up the cadence of their horn tooting.

"Joyce Gildea," she finally said.

"Those people behind us seem mighty impatient, don't they?"

She wore a silvery blouse with diagonal candy stripes. It had a high neck and a huge bow whose ends extended halfway down the front. Her blazer and skirt were a matching tweed, with the skirt length going well below her knees. There was a lot of shape in the little that I could see of her legs. Beside her was a brown satchel, the kind of leather bag that looked like a purse but could actually hold as much as a man's briefcase.

She was probably close to thirty. Her blond hair was parted on the side and swept back, exposing her ears. It was slightly longer than shoulder length in the back. Her face was an amalgam of extremes. Her nose was too long and would actually have appeared pointy if it did not curve down slightly at the end. Her cheekbones were high and prominent, doing little to downplay the puffiness under her eyes that one often saw on people who worked too hard, worried too much, or grieved too long. If she had smiled, I might have considered her pretty. She did not seem close to smiling.

"I recognize you," I said. "From last night. You were outside the police station. Right?"

Cars passed us on the left. Some of the drivers gave their horns long blasts. Others added shouts of obscenities.

"Sure. It was you," I said. "You looked a little different, though. That leather jacket and those big glasses with the blue tinted lenses didn't contribute much to your reporter image. If it weren't for your tape recorder and your nonstop questions, I would never have guessed you were a reporter. Which paper are you with? The local one, the *Dispatch*?

"Kind of funny, isn't it? Last night you had all the questions, and I wouldn't answer any of them. Today, it's just the reverse. Hello. Hello. Is your recorder here inside your case? If it is, I'll have to talk louder. Look, my situation is a lot different than last night. There is some business I now have to tend to before I leave town. I don't like this town very much. The quicker I get things done, the sooner I can leave.

"I need someone to help me. Someone who knows Bayorvale and has connections and can open some doors fast for me. If you help me, I will give you exclusivity to any story you want to write. You just have to promise not to print one word until matters reach what I consider a satisfactory conclusion."

She stopped drumming her fingers on the steering wheel.

"Two conditions," she said, continuing to stare out the windshield. "First, you will not hold anything back from me. I am not going to stick my neck out and have my head chopped off without even knowing the reason why. And second: no sex. I don't appreciate your mentally undressing me. So cut it out."

"Don't worry about it. You're so overdressed now, it would be a strain for me to undress you mentally. I have one condition, too. If we are going to help each other, you are now going to demonstrate your superior knowledge of the area and take us immediately to what you consider one of the better restaurants in town. I'd love to talk with you right here, but we're drawing a lot of attention. If we don't move on soon, we'll cause a traffic jam."

And then she smiled. I was right: She did indeed look pretty when she smiled.

"Somebody should teach you how to tail someone better. You're too obvious," I said as she eased her way through traffic again.

"If you didn't spot me until now, then I've been doing a damn good job."

I wondered just how long she had been shadowing me.

The menu at the Amber Restaurant boasted of how the establishment had been serving area families for over forty years. What kind of families? The Waltons?

The eggs en gelée tasted more poached than hard-cooked. The individual beef Wellingtons were pleasing to the eye, but the roast was not close to being done. I did appreciate the waiter's choice of a Cabernet Sauvignon wine. But you know the meal is a flop when you enjoy the wine for its own sake, and not as a complement to the dinner. I kept my complaints silent. Joyce was paying. She said she had a liberal expense account with the paper.

It took most of the dinner for me to explain my involvement in the Morrow incident. I told her everything, including the telephone threat and the man who had posed as Morrow.

64

"Had you ever met Morrow?" I said.

"No. I've visited Editions Bookshop on a few occasions, but I never knew who owned it. I spent most of my time browsing at the bargain table outside the store."

"You never heard of Morrow before this?"

"Only vaguely. His name kept appearing in news articles about committees, charities, and service groups."

"So what makes you think there's a story in all this?"

"You. Your involvement. Last night your name came over the police scanner. I heard they were taking you in for questioning. The dispatcher was told to run a check on you. I decided to run a check of my own."

"It's mildly reassuring to know I'm still newsworthy, if only on a regional level."

"They wouldn't tell me anything at City Hall last night, so I stood outside and waited for you."

"And you've had me staked out ever since?"

"I went home and slept a little. You were still inside your motel when I returned. You're not a hard person to keep tabs on."

"It must have been cold out there in that leather outfit last night."

"I wasn't really dressed for work. After I heard the scanner report, I left my apartment in a big hurry."

"Speaking of work, you aren't right now, are you?"

"What?"

"You aren't working right now. Keeping a watch on me isn't part of your real job, is it? You're doing this strictly on your own, aren't you?"

She pushed her dessert plate away after only a few bites. "That's all. I haven't felt this stuffed since I was a little girl in grade school on the day after Halloween. I always made the mistake of trying to eat all my treats at once. Too much of a good thing."

"Today *is* the day after Halloween, remember?"

"Yeah. You're right. You are also right about my working on my own. I'm on vacation. The whole week. How did you know?"

"I just can't imagine a paper the size of the *Dispatch* allowing one of its reporters to devote so much time to a story that, on the surface, promises so little."

"Does my kind of ambition strike you as stupid?"

"On the contrary. I identify with it very highly. And

with the lifetime of pain that ambition can bring you. I've
been in love with things magical since I was eight. When I
was nine, my parents drove over a hundred miles to take
me to a nightclub that was featuring the great sleight-of-
hand artist Dai Vernon."

I paused to light a cigarette.

"Even then, Vernon sported the mane of white hair that
has become his trademark. After his performance, my parents took me back to a dingy room to meet him. The dressing room was foggy with his cigar smoke. Just for me, he
demonstrated his classic routine with the cups and balls. I
was mesmerized. Suddenly, just before the climax of the
trick, I startled not only my parents but Mr. Vernon, too. I
grabbed both his wrists and held on as tightly as I could.
'You've got a ball palmed in each of your hands,' I said. 'I
know it. Open 'em up.'

"I thought my dad was going to throttle me right on the
spot. Vernon glared at me for a long moment. Then he
gave me the kind of grin that nine-year-olds usually re-
serve for each other. I swear that I saw the man shed a half
century in just those few seconds. He looked like a little
kid.

" 'No one's ever done that to me before,' he said. 'I've
performed for mobsters, politicians, millionaires, and roy-
alty, but no one's ever grabbed my wrists like that. Son,
you're going to do some astounding things in your lifetime.
I know it.'

"Vernon opened his hands. They were completely empty.
He invited me to lift up the copper cups. There was a live
chick under each one. His little prediction was right, too.
That same drive that gave me the arrogance to grab his
wrists also helped me to set the magic world on its ear. For
a while, anyway."

"Did you ever figure out the trick?"

"Never. And to this day Vernon refuses to let me in on
the secret. When I had money, I offered him impossible
sums to divulge it. When I was penniless, I begged him for
the answer. I've tried every way I know. I'll never give
up."

"Do you intend to apply the same kind of doggedness to
the Morrow case?"

"Let's just say that I intend to earn my money. My offer

to you still stands. Help me out, and you get to report the story exclusively, no matter how big it turns out."

"And if I don't help you out?"

"Then you may become a casualty. People with my kind of ambition tend to mow down anyone or anything that stands in their paths. You'd do the same to me, wouldn't you?"

"You already know the answer to that," she said.

"Then neither of us really has any choice. I have some ideas on where we can start working. I'll be interested in hearing some of yours."

She took out a notebook, and I took out my notepad. The waiter brought the check, and I told him to bring some more coffee, a pot of it.

CHAPTER NINE

When renting a car, I rarely worry about what my liability would be if it is vandalized or stripped. In Manny Wasson's neighborhood I worried.

In the dimness, I almost stepped right into the two-foot-deep ditch around the front of the house where Manny rented his rooms. I guess the ditch was meant to be a footer for a planned addition (perhaps a porch) that was never built.

I took a short hop over the trench and got close enough to see that the sign on the front door said, "Deliveries in Rear." I was not really delivering anything. I guess you might say that I was making a kind of a pickup. I made my way to the back of the house, keeping an eye out for other potential pitfalls.

After our dinner, Joyce had dropped me off at the car agency. The folks there promptly rented me their finest dented-up Chevette. Joyce and I then made a date for the next morning at a local pancake kitchen at an hour that she considered slightly late and I considered slightly early. She was going to gather information that, without reporter's credentials, would be almost impossible to get. My job was to interview the witness to Morrow's death plunge. He was not as difficult to locate as I expected. Sergeant Fetterman had said that the witness had been on his way to work. Joyce did not know of any factories within walking distance of the downtown parking garage. He probably had not been going to work at a bar; it was too near to closing time. I asked Joyce if there were any motels or hotels in the area. The only one that she could think of was the Bay Town. I called the hotel and asked if the man who had witnessed the suicide the night before last was still on duty. They said he was not. I asked for his phone number. They gave me that *and* his name and address.

At that time of night, I was hoping Manny would be up and getting ready for work. His light was on, and it only took him a few seconds to answer my knocking.

"Manny Wasson?"

"Yeah."

"I'm Harry Colderwood. I'd like to ask you a few more questions about L. Dean Morrow's death."

I wiped my feet on a nonexistent doormat and put my hand on the handle of the storm door. My brief stint as a desperate door-to-door encyclopedia salesman had taught me that the more you assume someone is going to admit you into their home, the more likely they will. Just wipe your feet and move for the door. They rarely ask for proper ID. The Boston Strangler knew that, too. I wondered if he had ever sold encyclopedias.

As Manny opened the door, I decided not to correct any mistaken impression he might have about my being a policeman. The two rooms he rented were not much bigger, combined, than my motel room. He led me through a living room that still had its sofa folded out into a bed. The next room was a kitchen and dining area. The table had only two chairs. He pulled one out for me. The place was sparsely but neatly furnished.

Manny was in his late thirties. He wore his dark brown hair shoulder length and parted in the middle. The hair had begun to thin at the part in the front. His beard was thick with no trace of gray, but the moustache was thin and wispy. He wore a long-sleeve plaid shirt. I could see that he also wore a horizontal striped shirt underneath it. The landlord must be stingy with the heat.

"I don't remember anything else."

"What?"

"You guys told me to call if I remembered anything." He walked over to the counter, turned off the country rock tune playing on the portable cassette player, and sat down across from me.

"We just want to make sure that we got it all straight, Manny. Exactly where were you when Morrow hit the pavement?"

His speech was careful and measured, not having any of

the singsong rhythm that often marks the umpteenth retelling of a story.

"Out of self-defense, I always keep my eyes and ears open when I'm walking through downtown at night. I like to think I can take care of myself, but who wants trouble if it can be avoided? This kind of trouble, though, I never counted on. I was walking on the sidewalk on the Eighth Avenue side of the parking garage. I didn't hear or see anything that gave me any warning, and all of a sudden this Morrow guy smacked onto the sidewalk right in front of me. Fifteen feet closer and that son of a bitch would have killed me, too."

"What was the first thing you did?"

"What would you have done? I looked up to see if anything or anybody else was coming down. Then, when I thought it was safe, I ran up to the guy to see if he was still alive."

"I know it's tough to remember, but did you see or hear anything right after he landed?"

"I know I didn't see anything. And I'm fairly sure that I didn't hear anything. You know how your eyes get when someone takes your picture with a flash? All you see is the same dot, over and over. That's something like how my hearing was affected. On that quiet street, in the middle of the night, the sound of that guy hitting the sidewalk seemed as loud as a gunshot. I kept hearing that same sickening, smacking sound, over and over. I can almost hear it now. Except for some traffic noises from several blocks away, I didn't hear anything else."

"What about Morrow? Was he still alive?"

"No. I knew right away he was dead. I didn't have to—I didn't want to—touch him."

"What did you do next? Leave to get help?"

"No. I stayed right there with the body. I flagged down the first car that came down the avenue. I told the driver to get the police and an ambulance."

"How long before help arrived?"

"It couldn't have been more than ten minutes. It's weird, the kind of things that run through your mind when you get excited. All I could think of before the cops arrived was whether or not I'd be late for work. I guess it's because the older I get, the harder it is to find a job, and the easier it is for them to find a reason to fire me."

70

You and me both, Manny, I thought.

"That's nothing to be embarrassed about, Manny. Even people who deal with crisis situations every day have moments when they think and act irrationally.

"Now, think carefully. Is there anything at all to make you think that Morrow did not jump voluntarily?"

"You're asking me if there was anyone up there with him?"

He scratched and tugged on his beard. "I really doubt it. As soon as that car drove away, I walked down to the corner of the parking garage, where Second Street intersects with Eighth Avenue. I wasn't sure from which direction the police would show up, and I wanted to get their attention as quickly as I could. You know there are really only two ways to exit the garage: a pedestrian's exit on the avenue side, the side Morrow jumped from, and a driver's exit on the street side. The other sides of the building are right up against two other buildings."

I had never seen the parking garage, but for now I took Manny's word for it. "So, from the corner you were standing on, you could see both exits?"

"Yeah. Nobody drove out or walked away. It couldn't have been more than a half minute from when Morrow took his dive to when I made it to that corner. When the cops showed up, there were lights everywhere. I'm sure they went over the whole area thoroughly."

They? Did he no longer think I was a policeman?

"Even if someone had slipped out, I would have heard footsteps. The echo is so loud in the stairwell, it would have sounded like a kettledrum. And the elevator, as you know, is out of the question. It's well lighted. Since the back is glass, and you can see it from the avenue, if anybody had run it, I would have known it."

"Were you acquainted with the Morrows?"

He had been asked that question before, and repetition had not made it any less distasteful. His answer was a quiet but strong, "No."

He stared at a spot on the table, and he did not take his eyes off it. For the first time in the conversation, I could see that he was doing battle for control of his emotions.

"They told me he ran a bookstore. I don't even read hardly at all. You know what dyslexia is, don't you?"

I nodded.

"Lots of things look reversed and jumbled up. The last time I read a whole book was over ten years ago. Even then it was a book I had read before in school."

I nodded in sympathy, but did not follow his reasoning that his learning disability would prevent him from knowing Morrow. Judging by the amount of calendars, stationery, greeting cards, and video game cartridges sold in bookstores, I wondered just what percentage of bookstore patrons were readers anymore.

"Come off it, Manny. There are plenty of ways you two could have been connected. What's your job at the hotel?"

He did not answer,

"I already know. They told me you're their night clerk. You get to see a hell of a lot doing a job like that. I bet a lot of people are willing to slip you something extra to forget what you see."

"Shit. Look around this place. Does it look like I make one dime above minimum wage? Suppose I did rake in a lot of money and have it stashed somewhere, do you think the clientele who shack up at the Bay Town have *that* much coin? Do I look stupid enough to be a blackmail artist?"

It was true. Joyce had told me that the Bay Town was not even close to bucking for a rating in the AAA travel guide.

By now, Manny was seething. I could see why the Bay Town had hired him as night clerk. He was probably good at stopping trouble before it started. He had not lifted a finger, yet I easily imagined him lunging across the table to do me damage.

"I didn't have to take that kind of talk from the cops, and I definitely don't have to take it from a guy who plays games for a living."

"Games?"

"Magic tricks. Games. All the same thing."

"How do you know who I am?"

"Fetterman. He dropped by earlier this evening to let me know you might be paying me a visit."

"He told you to cooperate with me?"

"He said I could do anything I wanted—talk or throw you out on your head. It didn't matter. He said you didn't know your ass from a hole in the ground, but you were harmless."

I got up from the table.

"Manny, don't assume you have more to fear from some-one like me than the cops. If Fetterman thinks you know more than you're telling, he's going to do everything he can to hang you. If not in connection with this case, then with something else. That little moat that your landlord has dug around your place is not going to be very much protection."

I wrote down my name and my motel number on a piece of notepaper and laid it on the table.

"Call if you remember anything else, okay?"

Manny shot me a lopsided grin.

"He's on your ass, too, isn't he? He's trying to nail you."

This realization pleased him no end.

"Why don't you just snap your fingers and make him disappear like you did the Sheriff of Nottingham?"

Manny was referring to a cable TV special called "Magic Robin of Sherwood." I had a cameo in it.

"You're forgetting, Manny, that every time I made the Sheriff disappear, he reappeared somewhere else, bigger and more fierce than ever."

"Yeah. Well, before you go, how about telling me how that kid made that jet plane vanish a couple of years ago. It's driving me crazy."

I hated it when they asked me about other magicians.

"He accomplished that by pure luck. That's what I've been operating on for too long. Pure luck, Manny."

I left Manny with his cassette of music. I stepped as care-fully as I could, but dammit, I tripped in that ditch any-way. Pure luck, Manny. Pure bad luck.

CHAPTER TEN

By the time I climbed up the elm tree far enough to see into Mrs. Morrow's bedroom, my hands were scraped and the muscles behind my left shoulder were cramped. I tried to figure a way to sit down, but they must be building trees differently than when I was a kid. I finally settled on leaning my nonaching shoulder against the trunk, allowing my feet to venture far enough out on the branch to give some relative comfort. I nearly lost my balance in the process. The tree had not been too kind to me on my ascent, so it was not hard to imagine all the ripping and scratching the branches would do if I made a quick descent. Not to mention the rude welcome the ground would give.

Mrs. Morrow had finished dressing and was now checking her makeup. I wondered where she planned to go at ten-thirty at night. While studying herself in the mirror, she suddenly cocked her head as if hearing something. She immediately left the room, turning the light off. Probably the doorbell or phone.

In a few moments my eyes readjusted to the darkness. A faint glow on the ground below her window caught my attention. Having taken such pains to position myself comfortably in the tree, I wanted to take a few seconds to relax and gather my strength. I then cautiously descended, groping for footholds and handholds. Halfway down I got impatient, so I jumped. When I smacked the ground, I muddied my sport coat and aggravated my sore shoulder.

After making sure the envelope of money was secure inside my jacket pocket, I walked over to the source of the glow. It was a piece of cardboard half the size of my hand. It was black on one side and treated with luminous paint on the other. I could not see it in the dark, but it felt like a monofilament nylon thread was attached to it. When I held the thread six inches from my eyes and moved it back and forth, it was barely visible. I wound the four feet of thread around the cardboard and stuffed it inside my pocket. I decided to see where Mrs. Morrow went.

I walked to the front of the house, peeking in every window I passed. The act of snooping did not bother me. I took unexpected pleasure, however slight, in my treetop spying. I wondered if I was a closet voyeur. (Of course, are not all voyeurs, by definition, of the closet variety?) I'll worry when I start climbing trees in yards of people I don't know and there is no envelope full of bills in my pocket.

The lights were on in the living room, and Mrs. Morrow was talking on the phone. When she hung up she was crying. She repeatedly slammed her fist onto the arm of the sofa. She cried tears of rage, not sadness.

I stood at the window for a few minutes. My shoulder still throbbed, and I got mud on my hand when I brushed my coat to see if it was dry. I wanted to leave, but I stayed for a while and watched her private sobbing. Was there some masochism keeping my voyeurism company? Quite a crowded closet.

Before calling it quits for the night, I wanted to check out the downtown parking garage, if only to see how close Manny Wasson's description came to the real thing. I turned the collar of my coat up, but it did little to shield me from the wind that whipped down Eighth Avenue. The coat was ruined and would end up in a dumpster before the night was over.

I walked along the sidewalk in front of the garage. There was no way of determining exactly where Morrow had landed. I do not know what I expected to find. A chalk outline or maybe blood stains? I looked up. The top level of the garage was much higher than I had imagined. Four stories of a parking garage extend a lot farther than four stories of a conventional building. Every time a car passed, I tried to pretend that I belonged there. But who, besides a Manny Wasson going to work, belongs on Eighth Avenue at this time of night? I did not relish the prospect of another encounter with the police, so I went inside the parking garage. The garage had long since closed for the day, so I had parked my car around the corner on Second. Any cars left inside could exit, but none could enter. Like most garages, the management had probably taken down the license numbers of all remaining cars and left little money envelopes for those who planned to leave after closing time.

Inside the garage was a glass booth with a chair equipped with foot rests. You could get your shoes shined all year round in this garage. I walked up the stairs. Manny was right. The echo of my footsteps was very loud.

At the top level, the wind was harsher. I took out my penlight and held it at waist level, hoping its little beam would not be visible from the street. I walked up and back along the wall that ran along the Eighth Avenue side. The wall was almost as high as my chest. I leaned out over the wall. There was no question that a fall from this height would have to be fatal. If Morrow jumped, he sure as hell meant business.

I panned the concrete surface of the garage with the penlight, but saw only paper cups, candy papers, and dry leaves blown up against the bottom of the wall.

I hugged one of the cement columns for support and pulled myself up onto the wall. I winced from the strain it put on my shoulder. The wind was gusting erratically, so I did not entirely release my hold on the column.

Standing on the parapet reminded me of my last bridge jump. I could not remember the name of the bridge, but the river was the Olentangy near Columbus, Ohio. That had been over two years ago. I had skimped on my usual deep breathing and cold water shock training, and as a result came close to losing consciousness before freeing myself from the chains, locks, and handcuffs. I announced to the world press (actually two bored local TV news crews) that my escape artist days were over.

I was now experiencing the same heightening of awareness as when I had stood at the bridge's edge, encumbered with fifty pounds of locks and chains. I became acutely aware of my body's automatic system of minutely shifting muscle tension to maintain balance.

I wondered what Morrow had focused his attention on as he stood on the same wall. Was it the softly lighted cathedral tower three blocks away? Was it the blinking lights on the four radio antennas on the mountainside? The iron skeleton of the construction project? Or was it the face of an assailant intent on murder?

The sounds of laughter and echoing footsteps startled me. I leaned my weight against the column. The door of the stairwell swung open as I jumped backwards down from the wall.

The three youths all wore the same kind of jacket. I hoped they were not gang jackets. I also hoped that my muddy sports coat did not send them the message that I was a derelict and, therefore, an easy roll.

I walked toward them, giving the inside pocket of my jacket an easy pat to make sure my envelope was still there. They immediately stopped talking when they saw me. As I passed them, I saw that they were no older than fourteen. They walked up to the wall I had just stood on.

"Yeah. Long goddam way down," one of them said.

I turned and walked back to them. They again grew hushed and looked nervously at each other. I did not blame them. I probably looked like I spent most of my time sleeping on park benches. I saw that their jackets were from their junior high basketball team.

"You guys hang around here much?"

They looked blankly at each other.

"You didn't happen to be in the area when that guy jumped two nights ago, did you?"

They shook their heads.

"What are you guys doing out so late? Doesn't your team have some kind of training regulations or something?"

"Fuck you, mister. None of your business," the tallest one said. The other two stiffened in anticipation of my reaction.

"Son, you just blew a whole twenty-five-cent tip," I said, smiling. I turned and started back for the stairwell. When they saw I was retreating, all three of them started slinging epithets and catcalls at me.

I did not think they were witnesses to Morrow's death, but simply were attracted there for the same reasons all sites of accidents and violence become temporary attractions.

Nevertheless, I knew that if I wanted to, I could later trace all three of them, knowing the name of their school.

The stairwell door closed behind me, blocking out their heckling.

At least the one had shown enough respect to call me mister.

CHAPTER ELEVEN

All I could think of as I turned the key in my motel room door was stretching out on the bed. I did not even intend to take my shoes off. I just wanted to lie down and stare into space and not talk to anyone that I did not want to talk to. At least for fifteen consecutive minutes, anyway. No such luck.

I swung open the door, pocketed the key, and reached for the light switch, but I never made it. A pair of strong hands grabbed me by the wrist and forearm and jerked me into the room. The hands immediately released me, and the whipping action sent me stumbling across the room. I tripped into the bed and went sprawling facedown across it. Of course, that is what I had in mind, but that is not how I wanted to end up there.

I rolled over and swung to a sitting position. I heard a thud on the bed where my head had been just a moment before. I lashed out sideways and caught my attacker on the side of the face with the back of my knuckles. It did not slow him at all. He flung himself at me, and his one hand found my throat. Breathing was suddenly next to impossible. I used both of my hands, but I could not pry his fingers from my neck. In panic, I punched wildly into the dark, with some of the blows finding their mark, most of them not. Only an occasional grunt of pain from him told me that I was hurting him.

His other hand joined the first, and the vise of pressure around my throat became unbearable. I tried to knee him in the groin, but he was straddling me, and my legs could not gain any momentum. He began to bounce the back of my head off the wall. My pain became lost in the weakness that spread throughout my body. I hoped there was someone in the next room and that they would hear the racket and call the police. But they would probably assume that the bopping on the wall was just a by-product of a good time.

My right arm swung at my side, weak and useless. It knocked over the lamp on the end table. Before my assailant pulled me away from the wall to slam me again, I felt the giant glass ashtray on the table. I summoned all my remaining strength and closed my fingers around it. I sliced through the air with the ashtray, trying to smash his head in with the edge of it. On my first try I only thumped him on his back. Ashes and butts bounced from the tray. Some of the ashes got in my eyes.

My second try caught him on the back of the neck and he released his strangle grip on me. I swung upward and caught him on the lower side of his face. He groaned, more from surprise than from pain. I lost my hold on my weapon, and it fell to the floor.

He did not lay another hand on me, but his strangling and pounding with my head had done their work. A warm glow spread through me. It was not quite euphoric, but it was definitely better than the pain I had felt seconds before. It was similar to the sensation when I was manacled on the bottom of the Olentangy River. I wanted to succumb to a sweet, long sleep.

My last thought before blacking out was to check my pocket for the envelope. It took supreme effort. The money was safe. I was not sure about myself.

When I came to, my hand was still inside my coat, clutching the white envelope.

"What the hell happened?" Sergeant Fetterman asked.

The overhead light was on. The lamp was still on the floor, its shade flattened into an oval. The door was propped open with the chair from the dresser/desk. A breeze rippling into the room stirred the curtains. Its chill was refreshing.

My entire head ached, and I touched the back of it, afraid of what I might find. There was a sizable bump, but no wetness from bleeding.

I swallowed a few times before I attempted to talk. I expected my voice to be hoarse. But it felt fine. The tremble in my voice was due to emotional, not physical, causes.

"Just happened to be in the neighborhood, Sergeant?" I asked.

"As a matter of fact, I was coming specifically to see you. Looks like I came at the wrong moment. Or maybe it was the right one. You tell me."

I sat up slowly and leaned my back against the wall, hoping that my dizziness would gradually disappear.

"Did you see anyone leaving here?" I asked.

"No. I passed some people on their way to their car. I assumed they were motel guests and not coming from your room."

I had no way of knowing how much time had elapsed since I had walked into the room. It could have been two minutes. Or twenty.

Fetterman could easily have been the one who tried to put my head through the wall. After waiting until he got his breath back, he could have flicked on the lights and helped me regain consciousness. I was unsure how much visible damage I had done to my opponent, but I saw no evidence on his face of having been hit with an ashtray.

"Wouldn't happen to remember what they looked like?" I asked.

"Who? The people going to the car? There was one man by himself. And then a man and a woman. Nothing special about any of the three."

"Boy, you make a hell of a witness. All that police training has really sharpened your powers of observation, hasn't it?"

"I've always been better at questioning witnesses than being one myself." One thing in Fetterman's favor—whether or not he was the assailant, the money envelope was still in my pocket.

"You have no idea who did this to you?"

"None."

"Anything missing?"

"I don't have much here to take." I made a show of checking through my wallet. "Everything's here. A big two dollars in the bill compartment. And it doesn't look like the room has been searched."

Fetterman sat on the edge of the bed beside me. He wore a white T-shirt and a navy blue jacket. "You going to heed the warning?" he said.

"This was a warning?"

80

"You almost got your head flattened. Nothing was stolen. Unless you're just a victim of a hit-and-run sadist, someone is trying to tell you something."

"Well, I think I'll stick around, then. I have a message or two I'd like to return."

Fetterman nodded.

"I talked to Manny Wasson tonight," I said. "After you talked with him again. He told me you're aware that I'm taking more than a passing interest in the Morrow case. Have you talked to Mrs. Morrow, too?"

"Yeah. She said you're handling her affairs." He looked around at the room's disarray and grinned sardonically. "You're doing a real bang-up job so far."

"I could be of real help to you, Fetterman, if you let me."

"Not *could*. You *are* going to help me." He leaned closer. "Get my message?"

Loud and clear. Everybody seemed to want a piece of the action. First, Joyce Gildea wanted an exclusive story. Now, Fetterman was unsubtly demanding all the credit for anything I happened to uncover. Unless Joyce wanted to write a story that was made from whole cloth, one of them was going to end up very unhappy.

"Are your superiors on your ass that bad?" I said. "That's why you're here, isn't it? They think you're wasting your time on the Morrow case. They consider it closed. But, as long as I'm wandering around Bayorvale stirring things up, then you can justify your own investigation by saying that you are checking up on the troublemaker from out of town. But now you want to hedge your bets. You're afraid I might get lucky and turn up something important. So you want me to give you everything I learn in return for your promise to let me continue unhindered. Boy, some deal."

Could he have further hedged his bets by roughing me up so I would eagerly be chummy with the hometown cop?

"I'm going to need more than your noninterference, Fetterman. How about letting me use your resources to run down some leads?"

"You mean like license plates and stuff?"

"Yeah."

"No, sorry. Every day we have to justify more and more our requests for information. I have trouble enough running down my own leads."

"Is it money you want?"

"So, now you're offering me a cut of the Morrow lady's money? No, thank you—although maybe I shouldn't speak so fast. I don't know how much she offered. I could be passing up a small fortune."

"No fortune. I did think it was plenty at first. Now, after this, I'm not so sure."

Fetterman stood up and walked to the door. "I'm just hoping you'll use good sense and let the police handle police matters. In the meantime, I'll give some thought to something you can do for me in return for giving you access to our data resources."

"Was what happened to me tonight a police matter?"

"No, I don't think the police should know about your little tussle tonight. Don't call us unless you catch a slug or get a bone or two fractured."

He flicked off the light and closed the door behind him. I did not move off the bed. I wanted to sit there for another minute or two, even though I was still wearing my sport coat and shoes. I fell asleep in that position, my back resting on the wall behind me and my hand still clutching the envelope of cash.

CHAPTER TWELVE

If the real heaven is anything like Pancake Heaven, I don't want to go. The latter is a truckstop disguised as a family restaurant. At nine-thirty the next morning, the waiting line was still spilling out into the foyer. I elbowed my way to the front amid a lot of grumbling from the people in line. The patrons were mostly retired men, so it was easy to pick out Joyce Gildea. She sat in the far corner in a booth. If looks could kill, I would be in the real heaven now.

The waitress was pouring Joyce a cup of coffee. When I got closer I saw that she had four packs of Sweet 'N Low crumpled into little balls in front of her. The waitress passed me before I got to Joyce's table, and she said under her breath, "Better have a good excuse. She's steamed."

I had no excuse, so I told her the truth. "I'm sorry. I slept in. I really did. The alarm went off, but I used the snooze control."

"My snooze control works for ten minutes before the alarm goes off again. You're well over an hour and a half late."

"My clock is a very expensive model. The snooze alarm works up to six times."

"Oh? What does it do after the sixth unsuccessful attempt?"

"A little white flag pops up and a recorded voice says, 'Have a good sleep. You deserve it.' Then it plays the Brahms Lullaby. Thanks for telephoning me. I'd still be asleep if you hadn't."

"Do you know what it's like to be the only woman here under fifty? Three men tried to pick me up, and two of them gave me the same line. Each said that I reminded him of his granddaughter, the one that won the Miss Pennsylvania Contest last year."

"Sounds like a good line. In about thirty years I'll start using it."

As Joyce laughed, the waitress made her reappearance. I turned my cup right side up, and she filled it in one steady, practiced motion. She winked at me when she saw Joyce laughing. Last night's dinner was just a distant memory, so I ordered pancakes and enough home fries, eggs, and sausage to make up a second meal. Joyce did not want anything, claiming that she had eaten breakfast at home. The waitress walked away humming, convinced that she had witnessed love in bloom.

"Find out much last night?" Joyce asked.

I wanted to ask her the same question, but since she beat me to it, I filled her in first.

"For one thing, I learned that my head does not make a very good percussion instrument."

I told her about finding the luminous cardboard in Morrow's yard, my talk with Manny Wasson, my motel room brawl, and my conversation with Sergeant Paul Fetterman.

"How much do you think Fetterman is going to get in our way?" she asked.

"Right now, he and I are operating at a delicate balance. As long as I'm an excuse for keeping his end of the investigation open, then he'll let us alone. But all that will end the second he thinks I've stumbled onto something. After that he intends to pick up the ball and run for glory. If I could only get him to open up and help us, I'd be more than willing to turn everything over to him."

"Or, if you could gain a little leverage over him, you might not have to do anything at all. And then I could print the truth about your role in all this."

"Leverage? Oh, blackmail, you mean. Isn't that a little risky? Even if Fetterman did do something out of line during his career, how do we gather sufficient proof to put pressure on him?"

"The same way I got this stuff." She unzipped her bag, took out two file folders, and handed them to me.

"Jesus." The first file was thick with tear sheets from a computer printer. At the top of each sheet was the name "L. Dean Morrow." The papers contained a dossier on Morrow, including taxes, driving record, real estate transactions, and the complete absence of any criminal record. The sources of the data were mostly state governmental agencies.

"Not much there. Look in the other folder."

At first I thought that she had done the impossible, that she had stepped into my domain of magic. They were photocopies, at least fifteen pages, all neatly stacked and stapled at the corner. It was the police file on the Morrow suicide. The quality of the copy was excellent.

"Friends," was all she said by way of explanation.

I'll say. Friends, indeed. I wondered just how good these friends were.

"It was just a one-time deal," she said. "A secretary at City Hall risked her job for those. Her job is still in danger if those papers fall into the wrong hands. She owed me. About two years ago I ran a series of articles on sexual harassment on the job. All my interviewees were guaranteed anonymity. City council put pressure on me to reveal the identity of the secretary who was the subject of one of my articles. I stuck by my guns.

"She promised me that she would repay the favor someday. A little over an hour ago, she walked in here with those two folders. She didn't smile or say anything. She just dropped the papers on the table as though they were a weight she was glad to get rid of. A two-year-old weight. She left without a word. We're square now. No more favors. In my mind, she never owed me anything at all. I had just been doing my job."

"I'll go over this later, okay?"

"Just don't let anything happen to it."

The waitress brought my breakfast. By the time she had emptied her tray, half the table was filled with plates.

"I ordered all this?"

She nodded. The excitement of seeing the police file had diminished my appetite.

"Help me?" I said to Joyce.

"Sure," she said, pulling the side dish of home fries toward her. As if she had not been enough help already.

The Pancake Heaven breakfast lay heavy in my stomach. I had the suspicion that all my digestive organs were holding a caucus to decide what, if anything, should be done in retaliation for my abuse. Joyce had long since departed Heaven, running what she derisively termed an errand, but what I preferred to call a mission. Actually, it fell somewhere in between and, like all legwork, would be treated with contempt unless it produced something useful. I was trying to raise enough stamina to leave, but I signaled the waitress for another cup of coffee. I was hoping that a big tip would make up for the way Joyce and I had monopolized the table this morning, but apparently the waitress was not expecting anything of the sort, judging by her comments about charging rent for the table. The glow she felt from Joyce's and my supposed avoidance of a lovers' spat had long since faded.

I systematically swigged at my two-thirds-full cup of coffee (the level had gradually dropped with each refill) and flipped through the dossier again, hoping to spot a new detail. The computer data told me that Morrow must have paid close attention to posted speed limits and he always used his turn signals. No accidents or traffic violations. Not even a bent fender. He was also prompt in anteing up to the government.

What I did learn was that Morrow had not lived all his life in Bayorvale. For a period of a little less than six months he had lived in the town of Somerset, about fifty miles further west. His short out-of-town residence took place approximately eighteen months before his marriage. The readout did not specify what Morrow was doing in Somerset. No occupation was listed. It simply showed a driver's license address change that was registered with the Department of Transportation. In this one isolated case, I wish Big Brother had been watching a little more closely. Joyce was out checking on what little could be uncovered from this quarter-of-a-century-old lead. Maybe she was right. Maybe it was an errand.

The police report was such a neat package, it might well have been tied up with a ribbon and decorated with a droopy bow. All the facts of Morrow's death were there, but with none of the nuances that were making Sergeant Fetterman fidgety. As of yet, my interview with the good sergeant was not part of the record, and I wondered if it ever would be. The facts in the report were in accordance with what I had learned so far from Fetterman, Mrs. Morrow, and Manny Wasson.

86

In addition, I learned that there were no traces of drugs or alcohol in Morrow's blood samples. The second time through the tedious data of the coroner's report, I noticed an interesting footnote. Traces of an as-of-yet unidentified petroleum product were found in scrapings from Morrow's fingernails. What product did *not* contain some sort of petroleum? OPEC nations probably declare a holiday every time we figure out a new use for the stuff. The report said that the results from the state police lab in Hershey would be forthcoming. Sure. All I had to do was pick up the phone in a few days and say, "Hey, Fetterman, where the hell's that lab report? Well, tell the damn secretary to lift it from the file and bring a copy on over here to the pancake house."

I closed the folder and got up from the table. Two busboys swept over the table like a postwar reconstruction team. I decided not to make an appointment to see Logan Zoller. I would just drop in.

The Closed sign was big enough to be seen while driving by, but I decided to stop at Editions Bookshop anyway. I parked a half block up the street and walked back. Editions was nested among a cluster of specialty stores. Downtown Bayorvale was another example of a shopping district being turned into a virtual ghost town by aggressive suburban shopping malls, and then further crippled by a slumping economy. I'd willingly wager that every store along the avenue had housed a different tenant each year for the last decade.

The bookstore was sandwiched between a factory outlet for golfing equipment and a shop called Wigs, which sold you-know-what. Wigs had gone to the expense of hiring a sign painter who specialized in the medium of Magic Marker on newsprint.

No gaudy sign announced the name of the bookshop. Small gold lettering told me I was standing in the doorway of Editions. I was also informed of the store hours and given a phone number in case I wanted to make an appointment. Below that was an index card taped to the glass, explaining that the place was closed until further notice due to the death of the owner.

There were no books in the display window, just a painting and a black-and-white photograph. The painting was a watercolor depicting Morrow sitting in a wing-backed chair. He wore half-rim reading glasses, and his face bore an expression of reverence. He was reading, holding the book as if it were a delicate stringed instrument.

The photograph showed Morrow and another man standing in front of Editions. Morrow had the same easy smile as in the photo above the fireplace in his living room. He seemed at least twenty years younger, though. The man beside him looked stern and imperious, not an easy feat for a man not much past thirty-five. His face had already developed diagonal creases that extended from either side of his nose the whole way down to his chin. To match his nascent jowls, he also had a portly build which was kept from looking pear shaped by his wide shoulders. His suit coat was unbuttoned, almost proudly displaying his ample waistline. He wore a tiny bow tie that was reduced to a black horizontal bar by the lack of definition in the photo.

The interior of the shop was bright from overhead fluorescent lighting. I saw no counter or cash register. A small desk just inside the door was probably where business was transacted.

I was not looking forward to meeting Logan Zoller. He had had at least twenty years to perfect the impatient glare that dominated the picture in the store window.

Zoller's neighborhood consisted of modest frame homes that were old but well kept. An unusual number of cars were parked on the street for this time of the morning. Few were newer than five years old. There were either a lot of jobless people on the street or a lot of retirees. The latter was probably the case because there was also a distinct absence of tiny tots and telltale toys.

Zoller's porch was elevated about fifteen feet above the sidewalk, the house having been built against a rolling hill. His gray home had been freshly painted, and there was no house number posted, nor was there a name on his mailbox.

I hoped he was still home. I had called fifteen minutes earlier, feigning a wrong number. Perhaps my phone call had not fooled him and he had been waiting. He opened the front door before I had a chance to knock.

I identified myself, and he nodded in recognition.

"Won't you come in?"

He did not speak until after he ushered me into his living room and had me seated on his sofa. He was as big a man as he was in the old photo in the shop window, but his shoulders had developed a slight stooping curve. For a man of his size and age, he moved with remarkable grace. He wore a three-piece black suit with a white shirt that had French cuffs. The loose, puffy skin around his neck made his bow tie seem even smaller than the one in the photo. Aided by the heavy eyelids that now seemed incapable of opening more than halfway, his glare had indeed intensified over the two decades. It was now a scowl.

When he sat down on the easy chair opposite the sofa, he crossed his legs. His hiked pant leg revealed a sagging black sock and a scuffed dress shoe that had never seen even a dab of shoe polish. The sole sported an oval hole with cracks around the edges.

"When you own something that is useful, you don't throw it away, do you, Mr. Colderwood?"

"What?"

"I noticed you were staring at my television."

My eyes swept the room. I did not see any TV. He reached over to a cabinet beside him and opened both doors, revealing a picture tube that looked more like an oscilloscope than something one would watch for entertainment.

"I've owned it for over thirty years. Never needed a tube. It never even had a warranty. Now, everything manufactured comes with a warranty. Why? Because everything is designed to fall apart in a specified time. The warranty is supposed to appease those people unlucky enough to have their products die before that time.

"I don't know why they stopped making them like this. It's a fine piece of furniture. Nowadays you walk into someone's living room, and you're greeted with a vulgar two square feet of glass."

"I never gave it much thought, Mr. Zoller. I never owned a television."

He did not smile, but his scowl softened a bit, perhaps in respect.

"I just returned from the Morrow home," he said. "Today was the memorial service for Dean. It was brief. Way too brief. But aren't all the really good things?"

"I suppose so. But some people today move so fast they don't even have time to distinguish the pleasure from the pain."

"Then, of course, there are those who have reached such a velocity that it is actually the pain in life that they seek out and thrive on."

"Probably makes them feel more alive."

"Perhaps," he said. "But it could be that pain is just a lot easier to find than pleasure."

He gently shut the doors of the cabinet.

"Wanda told me who you are and that you are now temporarily in her employ," he said.

I nodded.

"Her choice of words was lovely, just lovely. She said you were handling her affairs. Affairs. Get it?"

He laughed once, and it turned into a cough.

"Get it?"

I got it.

"That makes you her pimp."

I thought he was going to laugh again, but he did not. The last effort had left him more drained than five push-ups would have.

"You are saying that Mrs. Morrow saw other men?"

"Let's put it this way. Wanda saw enough men so that poor Dean never had a chance to build up jealousy over any one of them."

"Were you one?"

His jowly scowl returned. A bulldog in a three-piece suit.

"Dean had only one reason to be jealous of me. He was always in awe of my ability to make a dollar bill dance. Editions unfailingly showed a profit. If the shop had relied on Dean's managerial skills, it would have become another wig store in six months."

"Who were some of her alleged lovers?"

"Oh, I like that! Alleged lovers! Cop talk. You're getting good at it already. Every one of Wanda's men was nameless and faceless. She would not go to bed with you if she knew you. She didn't want to hurt anyone, including herself. The only one she wanted to hurt was Dean."

"That's why you think Morrow is dead? He killed himself because of the hurt?"

"Geez, she hired a real dandy when she hired you. I suppose it's normal for a guy in your line of work to look for

90

the gimmick behind everything. Does everything have to be so complicated? Can't you just see the truth without trying to discover where the wires and mirrors are? Wanda would have been better off hiring an accountant. Add up Column A. Add up Column B. Balance the books and get the damn thing over with."

"What you say is quite inaccurate, Mr. Zoller. In my magic career I've learned how to perform to perfection over a hundred and seventy-five tricks and illusions. I know the secrets of at least a thousand others. All these feats of magic have one element in common—the modus operandi of each is exceedingly simple. So simple, in fact, that when a bumbling magician exposes the secret of a trick, the audience invariably gets angry for not having been able to figure out the method for itself. My training as a professional charlatan affects the way I view the world in general. I rarely accept things at face value. And when confronted with obvious deception, I automatically seek the simple and direct explanation. By the way, I have never performed a trick using wires *or* mirrors."

"Never pulled a rabbit out of your hat?"

"Nope. Never even used a hat. Never saw anyone else do the hat trick, either."

"But surely you've sawed a woman in half."

"Sawed, chopped, guillotined, buzz-sawed, and mutilated with four-foot spikes. A real sadist's dream. I have even cremated some assistants. The real delight for an audience, though, is not the apparent harm being done. What they love is the miraculous restoration to health and wholeness. Yet, after all that chopping and sawing, the one sadistic act I have never performed is the malicious, vindictive assassination of another person's character. I do not believe a restoration is possible after that kind of destruction."

"So you don't think I should be so blunt about poor widow Wanda. You, sir, are about as subtle as one of your buzz saws. I take it nobody has corroborated my version of Mrs. Morrow's extracurricular social life yet? Don't worry. They will."

"You don't talk very highly of someone who is your new boss."

"Wrong on that count, Magic Man. You're looking at my new boss."

"You're buying the shop?"

"Don't play dumb with me. Surely Wanda told you that the bookshop is mine due to sheer willpower."

"Willpower? Oh, Morrow's will."

"Of course. Wanda will have no use for Editions. She loves neither books nor business. Her reading is restricted to *Better Homes and Gardens, National Enquirer,* and an occasional racy paperback that will provide role models for her own unimaginative love life. Dean was dedicated to books and book lovers. He knew that even though I don't totally share his obsession, I will continue the work that he started."

"The shop turns a good profit?"

"Nothing spectacular, but always substantial and dependable. I must say that it will do even better now. Many of Dean's ideas were less than income-producing."

"You seem quite pleased with your new position," I said. "I cannot help but wonder what heights you went to in achieving it."

"Certainly not to the top of the downtown parking garage, I can assure you. The transfer of the shop to me has been a part of Dean's will for years. And, before you ask the next question, he exhibited no intention, to my knowledge, of writing me out of his will."

"Did Morrow ever express an interest in the supernatural?"

Zoller straightened up in his chair. He winced at the movement.

"Owww. Excuse me. My back's been bothering me the last couple of days. Interesting you should ask about ghosties and goblins. I gave Dean quite a ribbing when he began asking me for books on the subject."

"When was that?"

"About a month ago. You see, that's how we get a lot of our business—from people requesting out-of-print books on esoteric topics. I have contacts. I have access to sources that Dean could never get. I never did get hold of most of the titles he was interested in. Do you think he was contemplating making a comeback after his suicide?"

"For what purpose, Mr. Zoller? To tell us why he did it? It would have been a lot easier for him to leave a note. That is, if it was a suicide."

"I'm convinced that it was. There's no question in my

mind why he did it. The only thing stronger than his love for books was his love for Wanda. And that woman made a mockery of him."

"Your mention of book searching has reminded me of something. I've lost count of the number of places I've lived, but it seems that every time I move, some of my belongings mysteriously vanish or become irreparably damaged. I've lost a small fortune in books and magic apparatus that way. One book that I particularly miss is *Greater Magic* by John Northern Hilliard. Even if I hadn't lost it—about seven years ago—I probably would have worn it out by now. I've never taken the time to track down another copy. I don't know how long it's been out of print. Could you help me out?"

"A book search is not cheap, Mr. Colderwood. Nor is it always fast. But I am sure I can acquire a copy for you. If I'm successful, you will not be obligated to buy it. I'll just quote you a price, and you can take it or leave it."

I agreed to the conditions, and he patted his suit jacket, looking for a pen and something to write the title on. I did not volunteer my notepad. He left the room to search for one.

My eyes fell on the telephone on the end table beside me. Its soft beige color and state-of-the-art features were in sharp contrast to Zoller's taste in televisions. Among the phone's modern functions was instant dialing. Half a dozen numbers were programmed into the system so that a touch of the button would immediately ring a predetermined number. Zoller had the usual fire, police, and ambulance numbers. In addition, he had Morrow's number and one marked "Pinetti." I hit the Pinetti button and within seconds was connected with the answering service of Dr. Andrew Pinetti. I hit the receiver button and was about to cradle the phone when I saw that he had two fire call numbers listed. I pressed the first one and a City Hall switchboard operator answered. I pressed the second and let it ring several times. I was glad the place was not on fire. Just when I was going to hang up, a man answered.

"Would you guys shut the fuck up?" a muffled voice said. "Hello. Hey, I'm sorry, buddy. Too much racket here. How much today?"

"What's that?"

"This is Fireeno's, remember? How much?"

93

"What number is this?"

He hung up. Then I did, too. Zoller returned to the living room, pen and pad in hand. He recorded the name and author of the book and was not dismayed that I had no memory of the copyright date and the publisher's name. He said he could easily look them up.

He apologized for not sitting down, explaining that his back was giving him more trouble than usual today.

"Chronic problem?" I said.

"Yes."

Dr. Pinetti was probably his orthopedic surgeon or chiropractor. I wondered if he had aggravated his back by wiping up the floor with me last night in my motel room. I did not want to admit that a man his age had bested me, but his size was considerable, and he did have the elements of darkness and surprise on his side. The same fingers that were now delicately curled around the ball-point pen could have been the ones that nearly crushed my windpipe.

I thanked him for his time, and he asked where I was headed next.

"To Homey's."

"Home?"

"No. Homey is a person's name."

CHAPTER THIRTEEN

The park where Morrow and Homey played their games was not exactly the calming oasis one hopes to find in the middle of urban hustle and bustle. In fact, it was just more of the same bustle, with fewer buildings and an increased emphasis on hustle. I might have been on the Bowery, judging by the number of requests I received for spare change. Except that these junior panhandlers were all dressed better than I and were clean-shaven or, in some cases, had not yet begun shaving. The section of the park reserved for preschoolers—the monkey bars and the mountain-tunnel maze—had been appropriated by these older youngsters. They sprawled over the playground equipment, striving mightily to make their posture-twisting positions look comfortable. Most of them clutched suitcase-size radios, possibly purchased with spare change. It would have been nicer if they all had been tuned to the same station. I ignored their begging, moving past them to the benches.

The women on the benches outnumbered the men by two to one. The pairings were according to sex, men talking to men, women talking to women. The benches formed a half circle around a grassy area. The rest of the circle was completed by a curved line of six trees. In the center of the grassy area was a white sculpted bust. I could see that the sculpture was of a man, but beyond that, I could not imagine what the original state of the bust had been. Graffiti and vandalism had taken their toll.

A white-haired man sat tailor fashion on the grass in front of the statue. He was making light strokes on a sketch pad in his lap. He did not look up when I approached him.

"Are you Homey?"

He kept sketching. Emerging on the page was a drawing of John F. Kennedy.

"Did you know a man named Dean Morrow?"

Still no response. I saw that the stems of the man's eyeglasses were three times thicker than normal, so I gently touched his shoulder. He looked up at me and promptly turned up his hearing aid. I sat down beside him. The grass was brown and dry, and I immediately felt the unfriendly chill from the ground.

"You can't sit like this for long," he said. "Fifteen minutes feels like an hour. I usually take just enough time to make one drawing. No more."

"You are very good."

"Thank you. It's all from memory. I have over a hundred more at home. I still can't capture on paper the way the sculpture looked when it was first erected. I was on the committee to raise the money for the thing. Took us almost a year. We paid the artist twenty-five thousand in commission. That's why I try to draw it every day. Each day I sketch it from a different angle, and each day my sketching looks a bit more like the original. By now, I feel like I own it.

"With winter coming, it'll be months before I can draw it again. But I've got plans. Little by little I'm going to restore the statue. I'll probably have to work at night to avoid attention, but I'm going to get the job done. And I'm going to see that the work *stays* restored, if I have to camp out in front of it. You know what the hell of it is? I'll probably get arrested for vandalism."

I asked him if he knew a man named Homey. He said he did.

"Did you know Dean Morrow?"

"If that's the guy who played chess with him, yes, I know him. I never talked much to Homey. I do know his last name is Hudson. I haven't seen him for the last couple of days. If you see him, tell him that he's a crazy bastard and that one of these kids is going to knife him if he turns his back on them."

"What did he do? Refuse to tip one of them for the privilege of using their park?"

"Want to give me a hand? My legs don't seem to want to uncross."

I helped him to his feet.

"Thanks. No, Homey did worse than that. He had the nerve to tell one of the urchins to turn down his radio. It earned him about a half dozen extended middle fingers. Incredible how many people have only read one page of *The Joy of Signing.* Then Homey surprised everyone. He grabbed the radio out of the kid's hands and stomped on it. His feet went through both speakers. Not that that made any difference in the noise level. The others just turned theirs up louder. But the people on the benches gave him a standing ovation. He gave us all a courtly little bow and shuffled off down the street. The radio kids were too stunned to retaliate right away. That was last week. Haven't seen him since. The kids have been waiting for him every day."

"Know where he lives?"

"Nope. Will you give him a message when you find him?" the man said.

"Sure."

"Tell him that if he's not coming back, to at least stop here once in the spring. Tell him there'll be a little surprise."

"The statue?"

"Yeah, he doesn't know. Just say there'll be a surprise."

None of the other adults on the benches could tell me any more about Homey than the sketch artist had. I found his name in the phone book, among thirteen other Hudsons. His first name: Homer.

Homey Hudson sat well back in his living room chair. The buttons of his cardigan strained over his abundant pot belly. He was bald on top and wore his wispy white hair long and combed back on the sides. A kerosene heater sat only three feet away and was aimed directly at him. A cat lay stretched out at the base of the heater. The cat reminded me of Homey—old, tired, and pleasantly warm. Two creases on either side of Homey's mouth gave him a perpetual frown. When they straightened somewhat into horizontal lines, I took that to be a smile.

"So, my artist friend was amused by my smashing of the radio?"

I nodded.

97

"His advice to you, though, Homey, is not to go back to the park," I said.

"Oh, I'll be back. Maybe in the spring. At least to see how the statue looks."

"Then he did tell you what he was working on?"

"He never breathed a word about it to me. Mr. Colderwood, are you aware of my relationship with Dean Morrow?"

"Yes. You played games together."

"To be more precise, I won games and he lost games. It did not matter what kind of game it was—board or card game, word or number game—I have the uncanny ability to second- and third-guess my opponent. I know his next move even before he does. This frustrated Dean Morrow. He even went as far as to read books on the different games, trying to learn strategies. But you can't acquire my kind of ability from books. It's intuitive. I think I was born with it."

"So you guessed that your friend intends to restore that Kennedy bust in the park."

"If the word 'guess' makes you feel more comfortable, by all means use it. But my conclusion about his sketching activity is no more of a guess than my firm belief that, out of that crowd of punks, I could seize and destroy the radio that belonged to that one particular youth and not suffer any consequences from it. If I had chosen any of the others, I am certain I'd be in a hospital right now. Or worse."

He pointed to a row of books on a shelf behind me.

"You want me to hand you one of those, Homey?"

"Yes. The third book from the left, if you would."

He fanned through the pages of the book.

"I don't read newspapers or watch TV or listen to the radio. My landlady told me about Dean's misfortune only today. It was just in passing conversation. She didn't even know that I knew him. I immediately took a taxi to his home. That memorial ceremony was still going on. I was refused admittance because I was not family or a recognized close friend. I sat in the taxi until it was all over. The meter was running, so it cost me a bundle. I suppose that sitting there watching the meter tick off an exorbitant fare was my way of paying last respects.

"You know, I'm not sure which game he was going to beat me at first. Perhaps it would have been chess. He was

98

getting so difficult to defeat that just playing him anymore gave me a headache. Aah, here it is."

From the pages of the book, he withdrew a wallet-sized snapshot. Holding it by the edges between his thumb and forefinger, he gazed at it for a few moments, then passed it to me. It was a picture of a young girl that could have been in any high school yearbook. She wore her dark hair long and swept behind her ears. With her head tilted back and eyes narrowed, she gazed into the camera with defiance and spirit. She was beautiful, and she knew it.

"Do you know who she is?" Homey asked.

"I was going to ask you."

He swiveled his chair until it faced the uncurtained window. It gave him a prime view of the liquor store across the street. He watched people enter and exit, clutching their little brown packages. I had a feeling that he spent many hours in front of the window, observing the never-ending procession.

"Dean and I were acquainted for about three years. It was months before we even knew one another's names. We just liked to sit in the park for an hour or so a day, playing whatever game I happened to tote along that day. I never invited him here, and he never invited me to his house. During the winter, we'd hibernate separately. When spring arrived, he would emerge as a slightly stronger player, more decisive and employing more complex strategies. As for me, I would be just a bit slower. Not less competent, mind you, just slower."

"Did you ever talk about anything other than your games?"

"Rarely. Our passion for play was enormous, although I think our motives were different. He liked to play and liked to win. I like to play and loathe to lose. That difference in attitude is more subtle than you think. My overwhelming drive to avoid loss leaves me with little time and energy to find ways to improve my play. Dean was constantly searching for ways to get better. In another three years, I would have been no contest for him, regardless of our chosen game."

The top shelf of the bookcase contained more games than I had ever seen outside of a toy shop: Parcheesi, chess, Pokeno, cribbage, Stratego, Mastermaze, Scrabble, and many more.

"Did Morrow give you this picture of the girl?"

"Yes. About a month ago. On that day, Dean showed up late. He looked like he had gone without sleep or had been drinking. Perhaps both. We played chess, but I demolished him three games straight, in less than a dozen moves. I had never done that before. I asked him what was wrong. He wouldn't talk. But he peeled open his wallet and gave me that picture."

"He didn't tell you who this girl is?"

"He just told me to keep it for him. As if I don't have enough pictures."

I looked around the room. The wall space above the bookshelves was lined with rows of pictures. It reminded me of how some restaurants proudly display photos of celebrities who dined at their establishments.

"All family. Every one of them. Children. Grandchildren. Great-grandchildren. I look at them every day, but I hear from them maybe once a year. Mostly Christmas."

"I'd like to borrow this snapshot. I'll probably get copies made. All right?"

"Sure. Be my guest. Could you do me a favor, though? Could you get me a copy made? A big one. I'd like to stick it up right there along with my grandchildren. Hell of a thing. I've looked at that picture every day since Dean gave it to me. I think I know that young lady as well as some of my kin. Hell of a thing."

The girl in the picture wore a plain white sweater. The blue background was pale. The colors had faded, muting the details of her facial features. Her smile was unabashedly sexy. The photo had been well cared for. There were no creases or cracked corners. I could not tell if it was ten years old or thirty. I carefully inserted it in the plastic picture section of my wallet. There were no other pictures in my wallet.

"While you're standing, my chessboard and pieces are on the shelf right there."

I did not argue. I had known that he would not let me go without playing a game.

The board was made of cardboard and folded in half. The chess pieces were hand carved and badly chipped. The white pawn was missing and had been replaced by an oversized plastic one.

I dragged the coffee table over between us. He leaned

forward as he rapidly set up the chessmen. He simply left his king's pawn set up two spaces ahead of where it should have been, indicating that he had already made his first move.

The first game lasted fifteen minutes. Homey was only three moves into his final attack before I resigned. The next three games didn't even last that long.

"Sure you don't want to play some sort of card game?" I said.

"Let's stick to chess," he said. "I know that you can't pull any of your sleight of hand over a chessboard."

But I did pull some sleight of hand. Between the fourth and fifth game, I palmed a fifty-dollar bill and slid it under the board.

He never saw it.

I think.

CHAPTER FOURTEEN

Her black Cougar was parked in my space at the motel. I pulled in beside it. Joyce wound her window down as I got out. Jimi Hendrix drowned out her first words, so she turned her radio down.

"It's an FM station from Pittsburgh," she explained. "Every day at this time they play an hour of oldies."

She sipped from a Styrofoam cup.

"I bought a tea for me and a coffee for you. I didn't think you'd be so late. I drank the coffee, too. Sorry. How'd you make out?"

"Not bad. I ordered an old magic book and played some games."

I told her about my meeting with Zoller and my session of chess with Homey.

"I also got some high school pictures made. I'd autograph one for you, but I'd say that the resemblance isn't too strong, and I'm about a quarter century too late."

I showed her a copy of the photo I had borrowed from Homey.

"I don't know her," Joyce said. "Pretty, isn't she? Why is it that people never smile normally for these yearbook shots? How do you know that it's twenty-five years old? Was the original signed or dated?"

"No. The guy at the camera shop figured that it was between twenty and thirty years old, judging from the degree of color fading and the brand and condition of the photographic paper. How did you fare?"

"Ever been to Somerset before? We're too late today. But tomorrow will be a nice day for the drive."

"Huh?"

* * *

Inside the motel room, Joyce described her efforts in tracing Morrow's doings in Somerset during those brief months some twenty-five years ago. She had called a reporter friend who worked for a newspaper there. He looked up the address that Morrow had given for his driver's license change. The *Polk City Directory* for Somerset indicated that either the address on the license was fictitious or the building where Morrow lived had been converted or torn down. There was an office building at the address now.

"Why did you call Somerset? Doesn't the local library have that kind of information?"

"The local library is closed today. They're closed four days a month now. Libraries all over the state are curtailing hours due to funding difficulties, but Bayorvale's outdoes them all. The community just doesn't care. There have been five temporary directors in the past two years. Each one was more of a yes-man than the last."

"So you think that if we were there in person, we'd have a better chance of retracing his steps?"

"A lot better," she said. "I've learned from bitter experience that the telephone is a poor substitute for face-to-face meetings."

"It's supposed to get colder tomorrow. I'd better check right now to make sure I have something warmer to wear."

I slid open the closet door and exchanged my light coat for a heavier one.

"Harry, listen. Right now, I'm not interested in additional clothing. Actually, quite the opposite. Although the subject of warmth is very definitely on my mind."

I replayed her words and then put my winter coat back on its hanger. I turned to face her. I looked for some sort of change in her expression. But nothing about her changed. Except for her unblinking, unwavering gaze. And the fact that the top three buttons of her blouse were now undone.

During the next hour we performed our roles to perfection. She as the eager investigative reporter. And I as—what else?—the magician.

CHAPTER FIFTEEN

Joyce and I both decided it just was not fair to waste any more of Mrs. Morrow's money on motel bills. She informed me that there was plenty of room at her place. I informed her that I hoped her quarters were cramped, real cramped.

The next morning was notable because it was the first time in many, many months that I did not run through my regimen of sleight of hand. Before we showered together, Joyce and I practiced a regimen of our own that I could only pray would become daily.

She dropped me off a block from the Morrow house and drove to her apartment to change clothes.

I knocked on three doors before I found someone willing to talk about Mrs. Morrow. The neighbor's name was Kay Rossi. ("Rhymes with moss-eye," she promptly informed me.) She was short and wore a housedress crawling with purple paisley. With her head full of curlers, she seemed to be wearing a knobby helmet.

"Do I know Mrs. Morrow?" she said. "Who the hell does? Nobody seems to. I've lived here for seven years. The favors I tried to do for that woman when I first moved in! Some people just won't let you into their lives, and she is one of them. After a while, I just gave up. Talk to anybody on the block. They'll tell you the same thing. That house of hers is just too big and isolated. That's the problem. I don't know what she's going to do now that her man's gone. You know, he even did the grocery shopping? Ha. That will be the day when her boyfriend goes out shopping for her."

"She's seeing someone?"

"For the last couple of years. Not that I'm nosy or anything, but you just can't help noticing such things."

I imagined Kay Rossi stationed behind one of the trees

in her yard, steno pad on her lap and binoculars pressed to her eyes.

"Know who the guy is?"

"Well, I know it wasn't Henry."

"Henry?"

"Henry's my husband. More often than not he was right here at home when Mrs. Morrow's gentleman came calling."

"Can you give me a description of this man?"

"It's tough. I can't tell you much except that he always wore a hat. Probably a disguise, right? A couple of times I thought I was going to have to call the police."

"Why?"

"Because he showed up a few times when Dean Morrow was still at home. I thought for sure there were going to be some fireworks. But nothing happened. Then I figured it all out. He showed up one night *with* Mr. Morrow. They were friends, right? Maybe business associates. Wow, some friend. Put it to your friend while you put it to his wife." She laughed at her joke.

I described Logan Zoller for her.

"No. This man was shorter and rather thin. From this distance, that's the best I can do."

I thanked Mrs. Rossi and gave her Joyce's number, asking her to call if she learned anything more about Mrs. Morrow's love life. Never once did Mrs. Rossi ask who I was or why I was asking such prying questions.

I walked up the street to the Morrow house. Rather than trek all the way to the beginning of their sidewalk, I cut across the lawn. After a minute of pounding and doorbell ringing, I gave up. Mrs. Morrow might be asleep. Or not at home. Or entertaining her hat-loving lover. Or maybe she was entertaining Henry Rossi. I found that thought entertaining. I walked across the lawn again and stationed myself along the street, waiting for Joyce. I thought I saw a curtain wave in a second-floor window of the Morrow home.

CHAPTER SIXTEEN

After minutes of experimentation, I found that there was absolutely no direction I could face and long avoid the wind's sting on my cheeks. Bits of paper and trash skimmed their way up the street, only to join other crushed cups and candy wrappers and make a return trip as a bigger mass of litter when the wind shifted. I didn't know how long the phenomenon could continue. I was glad Joyce picked me up when she did. I calculated that in another fifteen minutes the blowing heap of trash would grow to the size of a compact car and would probably have the force to blast a hole in Mrs. Rossi's house. Through which she could do all the neighborhood snooping she wanted.

The heat in Joyce's car felt comfortable at first, but soon became as oppressive as Homey's kerosene heater. I quickly discarded my coat and stowed it in the back seat. Joyce had already done the same. Her low-cut dress was stunning and made me glad that I was not driving; the amount of time my eyes would spend off the road would have made me a certain safety hazard.

"Admiring my taste in clothing?"

"Yes. If you had dressed like that earlier, our—uh—our acquaintance might have progressed a bit faster."

"Trying to say that I don't look much like a reporter today?"

"Yeah. Why the change?"

"Ever watch 'Sixty Minutes' or '20/20'?"

"Sure."

"Does Geraldo Rivera wear a three-piece suit when he's doing hidden camera work? Of course not. Once I even saw

Dan Rather go undercover wearing jeans and a straw cowboy hat."

"So you don't want to look like a reporter. What do you want to look like?"

"Your girlfriend."

"Oh. I see."

"Do I pass?"

"Yes, with flying colors."

She took the exit off Route 22 and got on 219 South. It would take us directly to Somerset. The ride was noticeably smoother on this highway. The Cougar ate up the miles as the rocky hills gradually flattened out into farmland.

"Girlfriend. It feels strange to say those words. You know the last time I had a girlfriend? I was a junior in high school, and her name was Betty Klein. We even went to the junior prom together. I bared my soul to that woman, and, let me tell you, Joyce, she burned me. Burned me bad. She made me a laughingstock. I never got over it."

"What did she do? Tell everyone how you were or weren't in bed?"

"Worse than that. She told everyone how I did my favorite four-ace card trick. Within weeks there were six guys doing the trick almost as good as me."

"Such treachery. You poor thing. That kind of heartbreak could turn you sour on love for a lifetime. You were so shattered that you spent the evening of your senior prom at home alone, right?"

"Hardly. Unless you consider doing an illusion show in front of three thousand people alone. By the time I graduated, I was well on my way to building my career."

"And Betty Klein?"

"She ended up, the last I heard, marrying the fellow that took her to the prom. He was voted most likely to succeed."

"In other words, he ended up a real loser."

"I suppose. I've lost touch. But the last I heard he was out on bail, pending appeal on his drug-peddling conviction."

Downtown Somerset was more stately and far less deteriorated than Bayorvale. Buildings that would have been abandoned in Bayorvale were freshly painted and thriving here.

We checked the address that was listed as L. Dean Morrow's residence during his short stay in town. The reporter had understated the situation to Joyce. Not only was that one building gone; the whole block had been razed. A complex of doctors' offices took up one half; a parking lot filled to overflow occupied the other.

Our next stop was the public library, which must not have been facing budget troubles like the one in Bayorvale. It was open.

After a few minutes of browsing through the reference section, I located a twenty-five-year-old *Polk City Directory* that listed Morrow. Six other names were also listed at the same address—all men. Below their names was the listing "Ethel Lents, proprietor." Morrow had lived in a boarding house.

Joyce found Ethel Lents listed in the current city directory. She lived only a few blocks from her former boarding house. No occupation was mentioned. We decided to pay her a visit.

"Mrs. Lents, my name is Colderwood. I'm an insurance adjuster, and this is my assistant, Miss Gildea. I'm trying to trace a man by the name of L. Dean Morrow."

"Magic business that bad?"

Traveling incognito has its difficulties once one has had network TV exposure. Ethel Lents lived in a high-rise apartment building reserved for the elderly. Before she would come down from her sixth-floor apartment to unlock the door, we carried on a lengthy conversation over the intercom that even included her comments on the state of today's weather. She was a slender woman in her late seventies. She wore widely flared slacks. Her hair was dyed a blotchy brown.

"Had you going there for a minute, didn't I? Surely other people have told you that you look like that magic guy."

"Some."

"We can talk in here."

She led us down a hallway to a room that was furnished with long leather sofas and cushioned chairs. A television mounted on the wall in one corner blared away. No one was there to watch. It must have been cable TV, because the woman on the screen was performing a seductive striptease. She was near the completion of her musical disrobing.

"This guy that you say I look like, the magician. What do you think of him?" I said to Mrs. Lents as the three of us sat down on the squeaky leather furniture.

"He's too cute. In my day, when a magician came to town you knew darn well what you were going to get when you paid for your ticket. That guy doesn't even look like a magician. He probably doesn't even own a tuxedo. By the time he and all those floozies got done with their prancing around and got down to the real business of sawing someone in half, I had already switched over to another station."

She sounded too much like the writer for *TV Guide* who had referred to me as "the Donny Osmond of magic."

"Mrs. Lents, my company is trying to locate a man by the name of L. Dean Morrow. Twenty-five years ago he lived at your boarding house."

"Do you have any idea of how many men lived under that roof during the twenty years that I owned the place?"

I shook my head.

"Well, neither do I. I never kept count. I used to keep count of the number that made passes at me. But even that number grew unmanageably large. I'm kind of glad I sold the place, though I was pretty broken up when I learned that the redevelopment was going to buy up the whole block. I changed my attitude real quick when they told me how much they would give me for my property. It was more than double what I expected. I considered it a sort of lifetime income tax refund for all the money that I've needlessly pumped into the government. What was that guy's name again? Morrow? Sorry. I don't remember any Morrow."

The stripper was gone from the TV screen, having been replaced by a pair of nude women sitting on a sofa, shyly holding hands. I showed her a copy of the picture that Homey had lent me.

"Know her?"

Her face showed instant recognition, but she pretended to study the picture, holding it at arm's length and sliding her glasses down her nose. She pursed her lips in what I am sure she imagined looked like deep contemplation.

Two men walked into the lounge, one carrying a bag of

corn chips and the other a litre bottle of root beer and some plastic cups. The one with the soft drink turned up the volume of the television, and they both sat down in front of it.

"Who is she, Mrs. Lents?"

"Is this woman in trouble? Did she do anything wrong?"

"We really don't know," Joyce said.

Mrs. Lents gently laid the picture on her lap.

"I never had much of a real family. I used to think of my boarders as a kind of family. If you get enough people packed into one room and get them laughing loud enough, you forget a lot of things for a while."

She stroked the corner of the photo.

"You really aren't an insurance adjuster, are you?"

"I'll be whatever it takes for you to tell me who that woman is."

"It'll take the truth."

I told her who I really was. (I actually felt more guilty divulging the truth than I had in concealing it. That is just another hazard of being a professional pretender.) I told her about the fate of L. Dean Morrow. I explained how we traced Morrow to Somerset. Then she upheld her half of the bargain.

"There were no high-rise projects for the elderly in Somerset twenty-five years ago. My boarding house, and others like it, often provided a bridge between your own home and the county home. More times than I like to remember, there were tenants that never made it to the county home. My place ended up being their last home. There are so many painful memories that it's no wonder I prefer to dwell on the fun times. In all those years, there were probably well over a hundred gentlemen who rented from me. In a pinch, I might be able to recall the names of twenty-five of them. So this name—what was it?—L. Dean Morrow. It meant nothing to me when you mentioned it. It still means nothing. But this picture brings back a memory that is as clear as if it all happened a week ago. How old would this Morrow have been when he stayed at my place?"

"In his middle twenties," Joyce said.

"It all fits, then, if Mr. Morrow is the one who was involved with the girl in this picture. Yes. Yes, I do remember him."

"What was the girl's name?" I asked.

110

Mrs. Lents's lips moved, but nothing came out. She tried again. Nothing.

"I *know* her name. I'm sure it will come to me."

"What do you think Morrow was doing in Somerset?" I said.

"Like I said, most of my boarders were elderly, or pretty darn near it. Most of the young people were buying one-way bus tickets out of town as soon as they had their diplomas. Unless you stood to inherit the family farm, jobs around here were almost nonexistent. Around the time that this Morrow was here, there was a rumor that one of the big suppliers for the auto industry was going to open a new plant here. They were going to manufacture car batteries. The hotter the rumor became, the more crowded the town got with young folk, all hoping to get in on the ground floor of a new industry. The city council and the county commissioners wined and dined the company representatives. Hardly a night went by without there being some mention on the news about the plans for the plant. After three months of publicity, the spokesmen for the firm announced that they would be building a new factory—in West Virginia, not in Somerset. It took this whole area half a year to recover from that shock. You would have thought someone famous had died. The young men that had flocked to town and lived hand to mouth, waiting for an ad in the paper to tell them to come to the Holiday Inn to fill out a job application—they all drifted away in a matter of days. This town seemed to grow old overnight."

"Morrow was one of those young job hunters?" I said.

Mrs. Lents nodded.

"Yes, if Morrow was the young man I am thinking of, he hadn't lived in that room for longer than three days before he and the girl in this picture started seeing each other. I remember how shy he was when he asked for permission to visit with her in the living room of the boarding house. I assumed that he had migrated to Somerset, like all the others, in search of work. He couldn't have had much money, or he wouldn't have rented from me. He and the girl didn't go out to very many places. Even if they had had money, gosh knows there weren't many places around here to spend it. Those two were the talk of the house. They made us all feel decades younger."

She shot a wistful glance at the men who were watching

111

the soft-core movie. They were as engrossed as two kids watching Saturday morning cartoons.

"On a few occasions she sat at the old upright piano in the living room and played popular songs. Some of the tenants would join in singing; others were content to listen. Most of the time those two sat in a corner of the living room, holding hands and talking quietly.

"The last time I saw that young man was the day before the story broke about the collapse of the factory plans. The evening that the news broke, I returned from shopping to find that a pall had fallen over the place. I didn't catch on at first. I couldn't understand why bad news about the factory would affect the residents that much. They were mostly retirees and already receiving pensions.

"I found the reason for their downcast attitudes on my desk in my little office. The young man had left an envelope of cash, paying up his rent in full, and a note saying that he was leaving. One of the tenants told me he had cleared out in the early afternoon. The young lady showed up to meet him, as usual, before dinnertime. She refused to believe the truth. It was awful the way she became unraveled. It took us a half hour to calm her down from her hysterics. He apparently had told her very little about himself. Not even what town he had come from. One of the boarders graciously offered to escort her home. I never heard from her again either."

"You're sure that the woman you are talking about is the same as the girl in that picture?" I asked.

"Yes. She made quite an impression. I still think of her from time to time."

"But you can't remember her name?"

"Not her first name. But I remember her last. It came back to me a few minutes ago. Fasick. I don't remember if it is spelled with a *k* or an *h* at the end."

"Mrs. Lents, please keep that picture. It might help bring back some more memories."

"I was going to ask if I could. I'm sure it *will* bring back memories. I don't know if they'll be the kind that will help you, though."

Joyce and I rose to leave. The two television viewers had finished their bag of corn chips.

"Here's the number of my newspaper in Bayorvale,"

Joyce said. "If you recall anything else, you can leave a message for me there."

"Oh, one more thing. That same evening of the day that young fellow left, someone smashed out every window in our living room."

"You reported it to the police?"

"They came and very nicely went through the proper motions. The broken windows weren't the first act of vandalism in the neighborhood, and I had no real proof that this Morrow fellow or the Fasick girl had anything to do with it. I never even mentioned their names to the police."

Mrs. Lents looked at the photo and shook her head. "They think Mr. Morrow's death was suicide?"

"Officially, yes," I said.

"Twenty-five years seems like a long time to wait to kill yourself over something," she said.

"Maybe that's what he was doing for twenty-five years, little by little," Joyce said to her as we exited. "Perhaps his jump from the building was just the final line of the final chapter."

There was a telephone directory in the lobby of the high-rise. I got to it first and looked up the name Fasick. In Somerset it was almost as common as Smith. With no first name to guide us, we would have to make some in-person calls to see if any of the Fasicks listed in the book knew the girl in the picture.

I got three dollars in dimes from the pharmacy next door. I dialed all the Fasicks in the phone book, putting a little check mark beside the ones that answered. As soon as each answered, I hung up.

There were twenty-one Fasicks in the book. Fourteen of them were home. Few of the addresses were on streets and avenues, so our next stop was to the Chamber of Commerce for a map of the Somerset area. We carefully pinpointed each address. With so many names, I was certain that we would be working well into darkness—unless we got lucky.

We hit the jackpot on Fasick number six.

CHAPTER SEVENTEEN

The name of Wilbur Fasick was, of course, located well toward the end of the Fasicks in the Somerset directory. But because he lived within blocks of the Chamber of Commerce office, he was the sixth Fasick we contacted in person. It had taken only a half hour to discover that, in this town anyway, there were two distinct pronunciations for the name. Some preferred the short *a* sound, making the name rhyme with *hassock*. Others favored the long *a*, rhyming with *basic*.

There were lights on at Wilbur's house, but they were dim. The porch light was off, and if a doorbell existed, it was well hidden and unlit. I thought that Joyce and I had approached silently, but a lady opened the door before we even had a chance to knock.

"Yes?" She opened the door only a few inches.

"Mrs. Fasick?"

"That's Fasick. Rhymes with hassock."

"Great. Wouldn't happen to know a lady by the name of Rossi-rhymes-with-moss-eye, would you? She lives in Bayorvale and—"

"Please, not so loud," she said, looking fearful.

"Mrs. Fasick, why are you whispering?"

"My husband's asleep. He works midnight shift and can't sleep during the day. This is the only time he can drift off. If he wakes up—just once—he won't go back to sleep. And you know what that means."

I could only imagine.

"Mrs. Fasick, my name is Colderwood. My wife and I would like to have a word with you."

"Whisper," she said. In a whisper.

I repeated my sentence, remembering to whisper.

"One moment, please," she said, closing the door ever so gently in my face.

Looking through the door's window, I could see three children huddled on the floor together in the darkened living room. They were about two feet away from the glowing television. I assumed they were so close because the volume was probably set at a mere whisper. Maybe they were denying themselves sound altogether. Gosh, how would they hear all the gunshots and car crashes?

Mrs. Fasick opened the door and came out on the porch. She wore a shiny softball jacket with the name of her husband's company printed on the side. I did not ask what product they made at the Dobyns Refractory.

"Mrs. Fasick, my wife and I are deeply involved in tracing back my family tree. We seem to have reached an impasse here in Somerset. The girl in this picture is definitely a Fasick. She is a distant cousin of mine, I believe. This picture is probably twenty-five years old. Do you know her?"

She opened up the door a little and switched on the porch light. She held the picture up to the light.

"God. That's Lou. This is her high school picture. Where'd you get this? You say you're related to her?"

"I think so, and I'd sure like to locate her. Do you know where she lives? Does she have a married name?"

"Lou and I used to get mistaken for one another in high school. We both had the same first name—Louise. I always wondered if that's why she started using the nickname Lou, trying to set herself apart from me."

Joyce looked puzzled.

"If your married name is Fasick, how were you mistaken then for Lou?" Joyce said.

"My maiden name was Fasick too. My people pronounced it different, though. When I got married, I just changed the pronunciation, not the spelling."

"Then Lou was no relation to you?"

"None that I know of."

"Do you know where she is living now?"

"I have no idea. I lost track of her a year or two after high school. We were never close. If it weren't for having the same last name, we probably never would have met."

"Did she have any family that you know of?" I asked.

"A younger sister. I only knew her to see her. I ran into

115

the sister once, maybe five or six years ago, at the Richland Mall in Johnstown. I introduced myself, and we talked for a few minutes. I asked how her sister Lou was. She gave me the oddest look, like she was suddenly sick or something, and she walked right away from me. The sister's name was Donna. I think she mentioned then that she was living in Bayorvale."

"Do you remember her last name?"

"I'm pretty sure it was Smith. They kid about the Fasicks here in Somerset being as common as Smiths. That's how I remembered."

We thanked Mrs. Fasick. She tiptoed back into the house to join her children in an evening of silent TV. I'll bet that when Mr. Fasick departed for work they turned the volume up until the roof shook.

"Just how many Donna Smiths could there be in Bayorvale?" I asked Joyce as we tiptoed off the porch.

I knew we would find out tomorrow.

CHAPTER EIGHTEEN

On the way back to Bayorvale, the rainfall never let up for a minute. We were forced to crawl at subforty speeds because the water drainage off the highway had grown sluggish. Every time our speed exceeded forty, the back end of the car swayed in a clumsy hydroplane.

The last five miles of roadside had been peppered with signs touting the quality of the food at a place called Hank's. Each successive sign featured a plate full of appetizing treats and a message that this one-of-a-kind restaurant was just ahead. But our appetites were whetted for naught. When we finally arrived, we found that Hank's was burned out. Not burned out in the new, psychological use of the phrase, but in the actual, physical sense. The place was a charred shell. The only thing untouched by flames was a sign at the entrance to the parking lot showing a young boy with his face buried in the world's largest hamburger.

But the road sign teasing had done its trick. We pulled off the road at the next Burger King, expecting to dine on a burger or two, a soft drink, and perhaps some fries. We got all that, and a magic show, too.

The back corner of the restaurant was roped off for the celebration of a birthday party. The little girl's parents had gone all out this year and hired a local magician. The props the entertainer had stacked atop his black nightclub-style roll-on table made me nostalgic. He was just beginning his show.

He cut and restored the same piece of rope twice. A black-and-white painting of a clown magically burst into bright, full color. And just when the kids all thought they knew where a little wooden rabbit went, the young conjurer turned around, amid shouting and squealing from the audience, to reveal that the pesky rabbit had affixed itself to the back of his tuxedo coat.

"It's almost the same stuff I did back in high school," I whispered to Joyce, in between bites of sandwich.

"Was your voice changing like that, too?" she asked.

"Worse. It vacillated somewhere in the narrow range between Truman Capote and Lorne Greene."

The cheers and applause at the end of the performance were unrestrained. I am not sure whether the young magician was more embarrassed when the birthday girl gave him a hug or when the girl's father called him aside to give him the envelope containing his fee.

I took a couple of minutes and filled both sides of a piece of notepad paper with cramped but neat notes. The young entertainer was still busy stacking away props when I ducked under the rope and handed him the folded-up paper.

"Good show," I said. "I wrote a few things down that might help you out."

He scanned the note and said a puzzled thanks. I could see he wanted to ask if I was who he thought I was. I walked away before he got a chance.

"You weren't too hard on him, were you?" Joyce asked.

"You kidding? That guy is every bit as good as I was when I was his age. If someone had given me the same advice that I just wrote down for him, it could have saved me two years of trial and error. Providing I had the good sense and a small enough ego to follow the advice."

"Would you have?"

"Probably not. Things haven't changed since then, either. I still don't have much good sense. My ego has shrunk, though. Maybe too much. But I hope that's only a temporary condition."

We finished our burgers. As we walked out, I saw that the young magician had abandoned his packing up and was reading my note. I winked at him as we passed, but he was so engrossed in his reading he didn't notice.

The rain slacked off enough for us to pick up our speed, and we made it back to Bayorvale in less than an hour. It took us even less time to load all my belongings from the motel room into my rented car. I followed Joyce to her apartment, and she helped me carry most of my stuff upstairs.

We checked the local phone book to see how many Smiths were listed. Since wives' names were listed in the *Polk City Directory,* we decided that tomorrow we would consult the directory in the public library.

I just hoped that the library hadn't closed down again because of lack of funds.

CHAPTER NINETEEN

The last time I had seen so many people waiting for a library to open was the weekend before our high school science fair projects were due. Over a hundred sophomores had converged on the local library in hopes, like all true procrastinators, that precisely the books and research materials we needed would be awaiting our perusal. Most of us had been rudely disappointed.

This morning the crowd in front of the main doors of the Bayorvale Public Library consisted of all ages and was of a distinctly ugly nature. They carried sacks and bags and boxes, and they looked like a vigilante mob from the most recent Bronson film. A hand-painted sign on the front lawn proclaimed that a book sale was starting today.

Joyce and I sat in the parking lot across the street. It was 8:27. And I was losing my enthusiasm for this case. I would have preferred to refund the rest of Mrs. Morrow's retainer, gas up the car, and take a look at all the country I had missed during the years when I restricted my sightseeing to endless backstages, motel rooms, and interstate highways.

My *F* in sophomore biology had done little to still the procrastinator in me.

"Why the crowd?"

"The book sale," Joyce said.

"A book sale at a library? They're hurting that bad?"

"Oh, they're not selling any of the circulating books. The books on sale are used, donated by patrons. They have a sale at least once a month now. It helps a bit. It seems to be the only measure the community responds to here. Other libraries have auxiliary groups to raise money, hold telethons, and pitch in with anything they can do to help.

But not Bayorvale. The only thing they want to do is to keep firing their administrators and hiring more incompetent ones to replace them."

The library was dilapidated, a former turn-of-the-century elementary school. The only noticeable renovation was a pair of glass supermarket-style doors at the front entrance.

"Why the fuss over a bunch of cheap, used paperbacks?"

"It draws collectors. There's always a chance a valuable book will innocently find its way onto the tables."

At 8:35 the crowd began chanting. I wound down the window but still could not make out what their chant was. Finally the crowd surged forward, funneling into the entrance. I hoped nobody got injured in the quest for a bargain.

After the library swallowed up the crowd, Joyce and I decided it was safe for us to enter. I did not look forward to the hubbub inside.

The main floor was deserted. A stern librarian at the circulation desk gave us directions to the reference section. I asked her where the crowd went. She informed me that the sale was upstairs. As we walked away, I heard her mutter something about inability to read. It was then that I noticed the half dozen or so signs, all proclaiming the whereabouts of the sale.

The reference librarian looked more like a salesman in a men's clothing shop. He wore a double-breasted suit with the cuffs of his shirt peeking out from under the coat sleeves just the right amount. His short red hair was parted on the side, and he wore a pair of metal-framed glasses.

When we asked for the *Polk Directory,* he gave us a quick smile and said, "Follow me." He set a brisk pace.

When he located the proper volume on the proper shelf in the proper section of the reference area, he stood aside, almost at attention.

"If the *Polk Directory* does not have what you need, I can show you other directories for this area."

"Thank you," I said. Joyce had already pulled the hefty volume down from the shelf and was flipping through it.

"This place always so empty?" I asked the librarian.

"Yes, pretty much. Per capita, this library has almost

121

the lowest usage in the state. Except for a new audiovisual section, our administration has done little to keep up with the times." He no longer stood at full attention, but he was nowhere near at ease.

"Too bad all the people upstairs at the book sale aren't down here," I said.

"You're right. However, many of the buyers are regular patrons. Have you met Willard Hollen, our new director?"

"No."

"He and his predecessors have made terrible matters even worse. Hollen's a real gem—when you can find him. He usually hides in his office and won't answer the phone. You have to knock real loud before he'll open the door. Other library administrators who are facing crises are hard at work galvanizing public support. And Willard Hollen? Well, Hollen likes to watch a lot of TV."

"It's a real tragedy," I said. "I almost lived at my neighborhood library when I was growing up. 793.8. That's the Dewey decimal number for conjuring and magic. Magic is sort of a hobby with me, you see. I knew that number by heart. Every day I visited the library, I made a beeline to 793.8, always hoping I'd see a new magic book, but always ready to pore over the old ones."

The librarian smiled knowingly.

"I have a lousy memory for names," he said. "But after a while, if you become a regular library visitor, I associate your favorite subject with your face. We currently have a number of 793.8s coming in. We also have a lot of 598.1s, 796.35s, and 929.1s."

"What are those numbers?"

"Snakes, baseball, and genealogy."

"Oh. When Joyce and I wanted to use the library yesterday, you were closed. How often does that happen?"

"Presently we are closed four days a month. We are so understaffed we have to close our doors just to straighten the shelves and properly rearrange materials. We simply don't have enough employees to keep up with it while we are open. Employees are running away from their jobs here. When I started five years ago, I made less than a first-year teacher in the public schools, and I have not received even one raise since. Plus, I am now doing the jobs three people performed five years ago. Besides reference, I am also in charge of interlibrary loans."

Joyce had closed the *Polk Directory* and returned it to the shelf. I could see she had written something on her slip of paper.

"Through a computer teletype system, we are hooked into a data bank which contains the holdings of all the libraries located east of the Mississippi. All I need to know is the author and title of a book. In a matter of seconds, the printer will spit out a list of libraries that have that particular book. Most of the time, unless it is a really tough one, a library right here in Pennsylvania will have the book we're looking for. Then it's just a matter of typing out a request for the book and hoping that the other library will cooperate."

Joyce handed me the slip of paper. It contained addresses and phone numbers for three Donna Smiths.

"Thank you very much for your help, Mr.—"

"Dennis Rockwell is my name. Glad to be of service."

He turned, executing a very smart about-face, and marched off to help all the 598.1s, 796.35s, and 929.1s of the world.

CHAPTER TWENTY

Bayorvale was too small to merit a beltway or a parkway, but it did have a stretch of four-lane road south of the city limits that took motorists from one end of town to the other without bucking side-street traffic. In no way could it qualify for parkway status, because the drivers exceeded the posted limit by only ten miles, as opposed to the mandatory twenty-five-mile-per-hour violation for true parkway drivers. Joyce was able to maintain a steady sixty as she threaded around the slow-moving compacts and semis along LeBoeuf Road.

"How many more blocks to Marshall Street?" she said.

"You're asking me? You grew up here."

"I don't have all these little three-block-long streets memorized. There's a map in the glove compartment."

"Boy, I bet you're hell when you're on your way to a police or fire call. Turn the heater off. Would you turn the heater off?"

"Why?"

"The air's blowing the map around. I can't hold it steady."

"Don't worry about it. Ooops—too late. Was that Marshall we just passed?"

"I don't know. I had my face full of map."

Using the library pay phone, we had located the former Donna Fasick. When I told her that we wanted to talk about her sister Lou, she had grown stone silent. For a moment, I thought she had hung up. When I mentioned Lou's name again, she did hang up. I was counting on getting to Donna Smith's home before she took off to avoid us. I had not counted on Joyce getting us lost.

And I certainly had not counted on someone trying to kill us.

The blue car pulled alongside us, matching its speed with ours. I pulled the map out of my face quickly enough to see that the car was a late model sedan and that the passenger side was pitted with dents. The driver wore sunglasses and a gray hooded sweat shirt with the hood up. He looked like a Budweiser tastebud gone hip.

When he slammed the side of his car into ours, I knew he didn't intend to frighten us. Just kill us. Quickly and efficiently.

Upon impact, both cars careened to opposite sides of the pavement. Joyce managed to keep us on the road, avoiding a mile-a-minute cruise through a crowded restaurant parking lot.

We passed halfway into the next lane before Joyce straightened us out. I was flung back into my seat as the car surged forward. The Cougar trembled in response to Joyce's sudden flooring of the gas pedal.

LeBoeuf Road was now a drag strip with two competitors, one of whom was playing by demolition derby rules. As we charged down the road with our newfound opponent, head to head, we were met by the blaring horns and screeching tires of shocked motorists who did not want to be sucked into our little game.

The hooded man refused to allow Joyce to pull away. We didn't gain an inch on him. The side of his car now looked like wrinkled tinfoil. I was sure Joyce's looked no better.

Just when I saw the traffic lights ahead, the other driver made his move. He slowed, letting us surge ahead. With a jerk of his wheel, he angled toward our lane. Joyce again floored the accelerator and hugged the right side of the road.

He mashed the front of his car into our left rear. Joyce lost control, and we spun around. I heard screaming and could not tell if it was her or me. Or both. With nothing more secure to hold on to than a crumpled road map, I closed my eyes.

I waited the wait of that long moment before the pain and the ripping metal and the boom of impact.

Her tires cried as she laid down a thousand miles of rubber on LeBoeuf. We bounced hard, and my head took a nasty shot on the inside roof of the Cougar. Something crunched under the right side of the car. Then we stopped.

No boom. No ripping metal.

And no pain, except for the bump on the head.

I opened my eyes and stared out the right window at the thirty-foot-high Freddy's Seafood Restaurant sign. We had missed it by inches.

Joyce, still gripping the wheel, was struggling to keep from sliding to my side of the car. The entire right side of the Cougar was lodged in a ditch.

Tears lined her face. I asked if she was okay. She nodded.

I looked down at the wrinkled map in my hands. The first street I saw was Marshall, the turnoff we had been looking for. I wished I had spotted it earlier.

CHAPTER TWENTY-ONE

Sergeant Paul Fetterman's son slammed the phone down on the counter, and it seemed years before his daddy made it to the phone.

"Where the hell you calling from, Colderwood? Sounds like a science-fiction movie there."

"I feel I just lived through a science-fiction movie. I'm calling from a pay phone in the mall."

I was standing right outside the video arcade, close to where I had done my last magic show on Saturday. The game sounds that filtered through the phone lines must have sounded like what a Hollywood sound-effects man hears when doing acid.

"My kid and I are building a shortwave radio. You're the seventh interruption so far today. The two of us are lucky enough to have a day off together, and what happens? Every stoolie and snitch in town starts dropping quarters. Tell me, what's on your mind?"

Stoolies and snitches. Nice to be classified with such wonderful company.

"You know Joyce Gildea, the reporter for the *Dispatch?* Well, someone tried to do a little reverse body work on her car today. They just towed it away. Before we called a taxi, we thought we'd give you a ring. The two cops at the accident scene told me this was your day off."

"What the hell do you think I am? The Three A's?"

I gave him the same description of the blue sedan that we had given the cops. Between us, Joyce and I had been able to recall three numbers of the license plate.

"By the way, Sergeant. You didn't ask if either of us was hurt."

He remained silent. Then he said, "Put the goddam soldering iron down, Eddie. It's not a toy."

"I just thought I'd let you know that, miraculously, neither Joyce nor I was injured."

He still said nothing.

"Also, there are two things that I'd like you to look into. First, the night that Morrow hit the pavement, did your men take down the license plate numbers of all the cars parked in the garage?"

"Of course."

"I suggest, then, that you sift through the report and see if there was a 1973 or 1974 blue Buick parked there that night. If it's the same beauty we saw today, it will have a four, a seven, and a two in its license number."

Fetterman grunted twice.

"One more thing," I said, pulling out my notebook and thumbing to the correct page. "Does the name Fireeno mean anything to you?"

"Fireeno? Oh, Christ."

I heard a snapping sound. It sounded remarkably like a pencil breaking in two.

"Colderwood, be straight with me. Are you involved in any way with Fireeno?"

"No, I just want to know who he is." Fireeno was the name the man used when I punched the button marked "Fire" on Zoller's phone.

"Jack Fireeno is a local businessman. His business is part of a chain whose regional headquarters are in Pittsburgh. The chain is nationwide, but their products are quite illegal."

"Such as?"

"Drugs, numbers, child pornography, prostitution. It really doesn't matter. Whatever happens to be illegal, Jack makes sure his people have it available for the right price."

I felt like breaking my own pencil in two.

"Oh. That's why you were worried. Rest easy, I'm sure that he and his people have nothing to do with the Morrow case."

Fetterman yelled at his son again about tinkering with the electronics project. I told him I'd get back to him later about his check on the license number.

When I hung up, I looked around for Joyce but didn't see

128

her. I wandered into Zippy's Arcade. Fetterman was right. His son's school must not have been in session; the place was jammed shoulder to shoulder with kids.

I found Joyce playing one of the machines. It was the kind you sit in, and it had a steering wheel and a moving road scene that flashed in front of you on a screen. A driving machine. From the sounds of the screams, explosions, and screeches, Joyce was not faring well.

When the lights dimmed on her machine, I saw her scrounging through her purse in search of another quarter.

"Hey, come on," I said.

"Just one more. I can't figure it out. How could I get out of that jam this morning, and then do so miserably on this dumb machine?"

"Because we weren't playing with quarters this morning. Come on, I'll call us a taxi. Then you'll see some real driving."

CHAPTER TWENTY-TWO

The three of us sat in the darkness of Donna Smith's living room, waiting for one of us to speak first. Even without the overcast skies, the pulled blinds and drawn curtains of Mrs. Smith's living room would still have made it seem like early evening. Joyce and I sat hunched over, ill at ease on the sofa. Mrs. Smith sat on a reclining rocker, the back adjusted to a nearly forty-five-degree angle. With her low-cut dress and two-tiered pearl necklace, she was definitely not dressed for housework. Her dark brown hair was almost as short as mine, revealing most of her ears. She was in her midforties, and apparently preferred smoking cigarettes in dark rooms to talking to strangers. That was all she had done for the first five minutes of our meeting. The room was so quiet I could hear the paper of her king-size cigarette crackle and hiss when she inhaled.

If we had been sitting closer and touching fingertips, we might have been holding a séance. Perhaps, in one sense, that was what we were doing.

"We're not interrupting anything, are we?" I said.

Even though my eyes had grown accustomed to the dimness, Mrs. Smith, sunken in her chair, still appeared to be little more than a silhouette. She dabbed her cigarette at the ashtray beside her but did not answer.

"Were you on your way out, Mrs. Smith?"

She ground out her cigarette, lit up another, and smoked it for a minute.

"You were the one that called this morning," she said.

"Yes."

"Don't worry about me. I'm not due at work until three this afternoon. I hate getting ready for work so much that I get dressed early just to get it out of the way. Every once in a while, though, I'll be all ready to get out the door, and I'll find myself dialing the number at work and calling in sick. A few times lately, I haven't even bothered to call. I just don't show up. I get real comfortable in this chair here, enjoying a cigarette and a drink or two, and I just can't think of one good reason to get up and leave the house. Ever happen to you?"

I hesitated, but Joyce jumped in and said, "Yes. Sure. All the time."

I looked at my watch. Mrs. Smith was not due at work for two hours.

"So you're the one that called and asked me those strange questions?"

"Yes. You told us on the phone that you were Louise Fasick's sister," I said.

"Took you long enough to get here."

"We had a bit of a mishap on the way over. Joyce and I are afraid that it may have to do with, as you put it, some of the strange questions we've been asking. We hope you can help us."

"Simple solution to your problem," Mrs. Smith said. "Just don't ask the questions."

"But if we don't, someone else will. And the consequences could be decidedly unpleasant for you, much worse than for Joyce and me this morning."

I lit up a cigarette and noticed that my hands were soiled. I hadn't washed them after our accident. I decided to let Mrs. Smith talk. I sensed she was struggling to find the right way to begin.

"I knew right after you called me that I wasn't going in to work today. They've threatened to fire me, but they know I've had other job offers. They put up with me because they know it will be hard to find someone else who will consent to being assistant manager of a complete fraud."

"Fraud?" Joyce said.

"Oh, our business is perfectly legal. And perfectly

unethical. I'm the assistant manager of Slim-Mart in the mall. I know you've never been there; people that look like you aren't our regular customers. Our patrons range from the pleasantly chubby to the morbidly obese. Half our products don't work, and the other half are under investigation by the FDA. Our manager weighs two hundred and sixty pounds. You'd think that her size wouldn't be a good advertisement for the store, but the overweight customers really identify with her. They talk to her about weight problems. Nobody seems to mind that she has gained twenty pounds for every year she's been manager. I can't even figure out why Betty is so heavy.

"We eat lunch together, and she never has one bite more than me, sometimes less. The manager of the restaurant we often go to calls us the Before and After Twins."

"Doesn't sound like you're bucking for the manager's job," I said.

"I'm bucking for the weekly paycheck, that's all. Now I'm wondering how long that will all last. Every time we pull the gate down at closing time, I think it might be for the last time. Business has really taken a nose dive in the last six months. Maybe it's the recession."

I waited for her to continue, but it seemed she no longer wanted to avoid talking about her sister and was waiting for me to broach the subject again. I pulled yet another copy of the Louise Fasick picture from my pocket. I showed it to Mrs. Smith and then placed it on the coffee table in front of me.

Mrs. Smith reached into her purse and removed a billfold. She slid a photo from the plastic section and laid it beside the other picture. It was a duplicate. Except that hers was creased and faded.

"Lou wouldn't approve of me toting her picture around like this," she said.

"Where is Lou now?" Joyce said.

"You really don't know, do you?"

I shook my head. I glanced back and forth several times between the photos and Mrs. Smith, trying to detect some resemblance between her and her sister. Both their faces were long, accentuated by eyes that were too close together, but any similarity stopped there. The yearbook portrait almost glowed with the smile that wrinkled Lou Fasick's face. Mrs. Smith had not come within a mile of smiling so far today.

"Lou's been dead for twenty-two years. She killed herself. Hung herself with some bed sheets. You better tell me what the hell you're doing with her picture."

CHAPTER TWENTY-THREE

I suppose I could have sung while Joyce danced. Then Joyce could have sung while I danced. But we had performed our little road show too many times lately. I settled for the truth, plain and simple, doing my best to relax while I told it. Sometimes the truth will set you free. Sometimes it's a pain in the ass. Mrs. Smith listened passively while I told of Morrow's untimely death.

"I remember reading something in the paper about this Morrow," Mrs. Smith said. "Lots of people just read the sports page or the comics. Me, I turn right away to Ann Landers and then to the horoscope. Occasionally a headline or two will catch my eye. Yeah, I remember reading about a guy jumping off a building. Morrow was—?"

"—connected with your sister? Yes, we have good reason to believe that. Twenty-five years ago, back in Somerset, did your sister have a boyfriend that you knew of?"

"Yes. Lou tried to hide it. But the whole family—Mom, Dad, and I—knew. Lou was two years older than me. She got a job right out of high school at a shoe factory in Somerset. She didn't make enough money to move out of the house, but she made enough to feel damn independent. At night, she began to leave the house earlier and earlier and stay out later and later. My parents worried and talked privately about it. They had always prided themselves on the open and honest relationship they had with each other and their two daughters. It was inconceivable that one of *their* children was locking them out of her life. They even approached me to spy on Lou.

"Even if I had known the details of her affair, I wouldn't have said anything. But Lou never did tell me a thing. Once I asked her point-blank if she was seeing a man. She

134

gave me an evasive answer. Besides being my only sister, I considered her my best friend. Was I hurt that she didn't confide in me? Hell, no. I hugged her and told her that I hoped to meet him someday.

"Her evening absences grew more frequent and longer. I knew that Dad was planning to do something drastic if Lou wasn't more forthcoming.

"He never got his chance. One night, Lou didn't come home. All three of us stayed up waiting. Finally, one of us got the bright idea to check her room. There was a note that simply and eloquently declared her love for us all. For reasons that were deeply personal, she explained, she would be absent from the household for a time. So few of her belongings were missing from the room, we concluded that she surely would not be gone long. The police told us there was little they could do. The note clearly indicated that her going away was of her own free will. She was an adult. It was a family matter we would have to handle privately.

"It was nearly a year before Lou waltzed back into our lives. Several times my dad was on the verge of hiring a private detective, but my mother always vetoed the idea. Mom wanted Lou to come back for the same reason she had left: because she wanted to."

"When Lou returned, did she tell you why she left? What did she do during her absence?" I asked.

"Lou was totally changed when she returned. It was hard enough to get her to talk about the weather, let alone the mystery of her missing year. She stayed in her room most of the time, reading books and magazines. She listened to records. But only old ones, the ones she owned before her year's absence. She never played any of my new records. Her personal appearance went to hell. It was embarrassing to remind her to take a bath or to change the clothes she had been wearing for the last four days."

"Did Lou see a psychiatrist?" Joyce said.

"I don't think there were any in Somerset then. Dad often suggested that we take her to Pittsburgh or Philadelphia to see a specialist. I think, though, in the back of his mind he was afraid that she'd end up in what he called a nuthouse.

"But she did anyway. It was a cold February morning—a Saturday I'll never forget. The policeman pounding on the

135

front door got us all up. I remember stumbling over something on the living room floor on the way to the front door. The policeman covered up his embarrassment with formal speech. He said he was sorry to inform us that Lou was in police custody, that we could come down to see her, and that we should also bring along a change of clothes. I switched on the light and saw that it was Lou's clothing I had tripped over. It was piled up in the living room, underwear and all.

"The police had received a call from a priest at a church ten blocks away from our house. He had discovered Lou sitting quietly in a pew at the front of his church. She wouldn't answer any questions. She just stared straight ahead at the altar. She was nude. When the police came, she wouldn't talk to them, either. When they took her to the station, someone there recognized her. Under the law, Lou had to be held for a thirty-day period pending a psychiatric examination. She maintained her stony silence that whole month. The examining psychiatrists found ample reason for her to be committed to the state hospital.

"We all lived under the illusion that Lou was receiving expert care at the hospital and that her release would be speedy. She never made it home. The hospital was only fifteen miles away, so I was able to visit frequently. During each visit I found her condition to be the same or a little worse. It never improved. Except for one day.

"It was in the middle of July, and I couldn't believe my ears when Lou cheerfully greeted me by name. It was the first time she had spoken to me since she had been committed back in February. I didn't even stop to question her sudden change. I just was overjoyed to have the real Lou back. Like two friends who hadn't seen each other for years, we sat in the solarium of the hospital until after dark, laughing and joking and avoiding talking about the fact that she was dressed in hospital clothes and would not be going home with me that night. I was sure that it was just a matter of time before the staff took note of her miraculous progress, and that Lou would soon be riding out through the iron gates with me."

Mrs. Smith poked a finger inside her flat cigarette pack, making sure it was empty. I offered her one of mine, and she accepted.

"That last half hour of the last time that we talked, Lou

got real solemn. She told me why she had left home. She had become pregnant, and she had been deserted by her lover. The rage and shame was too much for her. She wanted to be alone to have her baby."

"Did her boyfriend know she was pregnant?" Joyce asked.

"She never even told me her boyfriend's name, but she did say that she got no chance to tell him she was expecting. She said he just left town with no good-byes. Perhaps his seriousness about their love affair did not match Lou's, and he panicked when he suspected she was pregnant. Or maybe his departure was just ill timed, for other reasons altogether."

I offered a reason. "One possibility might simply be that he was in town to try to get employment with that proposed battery factory. When the plans fell through, he might have left town like the scores of other hopeful young men."

"The battery factory?" Mrs. Smith said. "Was that at the same time when Lou ran away? Whatever his reasons, Lou was crushed by his leaving. She was *too* damn independent, that's all. If she had come to the rest of us for help, we might have all worked it out together.

"That night at the hospital, I was so overjoyed at her finally opening up, I didn't press for any details of her absence. I thought there'd be time for all that later. During the last five minutes of our visit, though, I realized that I should have tried to learn more. But the hospital staff was getting nasty about my staying past visiting hours. I quickly asked Lou about her baby. Where was it? Was it a boy or a girl? She told me it was the birthday of the child on that day, the day of my visit. That accounted for her mysterious opening up.

"As I was leaving, she said four words—the last I ever heard her say. 'I killed it, Donna,' she said. The orderlies were practically dragging me away as I bombarded her with questions. 'How did you kill it? Why?' Then she became as silent as before.

"I had my hopes up for my next visit, but it was like trying to talk to a piece of furniture. Trying to find someone at the hospital who would even listen to my story of Lou's sudden lucid behavior was a study in government bureaucracy. Before long, I discovered the real purpose of the hos-

137

pital. It wasn't there to help anyone. It was just a prison whose inmates were convicted of the unpardonable crime of not being able to cope with the outside world. In many cases their sentences were for life.

"I saw Lou about twenty times during the next year. As the anniversary date of her talking spree approached, my hopes soared. Maybe she would again choose the birthday of her baby to communicate with me. The day finally came, and I was psyched up.

"When I arrived, the lady at the reception desk asked for my name three separate times. Then she requested an ID. That had never happened before. She gave me an office number and said I was to report there. One of the administrators wanted to talk to me. I can't remember his name or what level he was on the hospital hierarchy. But you can bet he was low man on their totem pole. He had been charged with the unpleasant task of informing me that Lou had been found two hours before, swinging back and forth in her room. She had tied a bed sheet around her neck. That day I vowed to find the man that was responsible for her death."

"Didn't find him, did you?" I asked.

"Funny how vows get twisted around. Even wedding vows. I vowed to find the man that hurt my sister. Instead I found a man of my own, one that would hurt me. My mission got sidetracked rather early by my own personal problems."

She told me she got married not long after Lou's death. It was ironic that she was unable to have children after her sister had killed herself over bearing a child. Not long after Mrs. Smith and her husband stopped trying to have children, they also stopped trying to have a marriage. Her husband remarried shortly after the divorce.

"He has a new wife, a new home, and a life full of kids. And I have . . . what do I have? I have two strangers in my living room asking personal questions to which I have responded much too freely."

She looked at her wristwatch.

"No. I definitely don't think I'm going to make it to work. Maybe I'll just sit in this chair for another hour or two or three. How's that for an exciting day?"

"Mrs. Smith. One question. If you don't answer it, I can almost guarantee that a police detective named Fetterman will ask the very same question. Where were you between midnight and two A.M. this past Sunday morning?"

"Sunday morning? Oh, that's when you said this Morrow jumped from the building. You know, that's a couple of days ago, but it might just as well be a couple of months. I was probably sitting on this very chair, with the television playing too loud and with four drinks too many swimming around inside me. Yeah, if it was this weekend—or any weekend, for that matter—I'm sure that's what I was doing."

"Can you—"

"Prove it? Hell, no. Mr. Colderwood, if I had known the identity of my sister's lover twenty years ago, I might have gone off half-cocked and done something drastic, much worse than nudging someone off a building top. Rest assured I'd have an ironclad alibi, too. But at the present time it is going to take several hours before I'm able to dredge up a discernible, genuine feeling about the affair. Hours of contemplation. You and Miss Gildea care to join me in a few glasses of contemplation?"

We politely declined the offer. We showed ourselves out, leaving her in her chair, staring blankly ahead, where I'm sure she was on the night L. Dean Morrow took his fatal plunge.

CHAPTER TWENTY-FOUR

The windshield wipers of my rented Chevette threatened to lay down and die with every sweep. I marveled at the workmanship of the wiper blades. Must be handmade. Could it be sheer accident that the rubber was nonexistent in exactly the area that I needed to see safely through the windshield?

"Turn here, Harry. Geez, missed it again," Joyce said.

It was the third time I had missed. Our trip back to Joyce's apartment was becoming a grand tour of Bayorvale's side streets. In order to see through the clear sections of the windshield, I had to lean forward and tilt my head back in an orthopedically unsound position. I wished we had used the taxi all afternoon.

"You sure you know where we are?" I asked. "I think we've passed that store before."

"No. That store's part of a chain. They're all over this part of the state. One every four square blocks."

"Couldn't they think of a more original name? How can you have faith in a convenience store named Mom and Pop?"

Joyce's reply was a long hoarse cough.

"Catching cold?"

"I don't think so. Must be this damp weather. Talking to Mrs. Smith brought me down, too."

I agreed. I felt as bewildered as a little kid who had thrown away the instructions to a model airplane, only to discover himself lost in a jumble of half-glued parts.

My knuckles went white every time a car pulled abreast of us. The Chevette did not have the pickup to outdistance anyone, so I applied the brakes, letting each passer zip by. I didn't want a repeat of this morning's drag race.

"Do you believe Donna Smith's story?" she asked.

"I don't know. There's a lot of it we could double-check."

"There have been some big shake-ups in the state hospital system in the last few years. Even if we could get access to their records, I'm not sure if they'd have detailed files on something so long ago."

"And even if Mrs. Smith is telling the truth, it's still up in the air as to whether her sister told *her* the truth."

"You mean about killing the baby?"

"Yeah. Killing her baby. If she even had one in the first place."

I was apprehensive about leaving Mrs. Smith in her foggy state of depression and gloom. Even though I peeked inside her garage and saw that her Grenada did not remotely resemble the car that ran us off the road, it did not take much imagination to envision her tooling down the highway, sideswiping anyone who did not strike her fancy. Anger and resentment seethed inside her. Other than his hooded sweat shirt, how much had I seen of the hit-and-run driver? How certain was I that it was a man?

A red Road Runner pulled up alongside us on the left. It was decorated with stripes and excess chrome. Even in this sloppy weather, it retained its gloss and shine. It was filled to overflow with teenagers. Somehow one of them found enough elbow room to crank down his window and pitch a beer can our way. It missed, sailing over our roof. Exceeding the decibel level of a bulldozer, the Road Runner accelerated, fishtailed slightly, and roared ahead, losing us in its mist.

I glanced at Joyce. Her head was tilted back, eyes closed. Asleep. I pulled over and checked the street map of Bayorvale I had taken from her car before the tow truck did its work. In a moment I got my bearings and plotted a direct course to her apartment.

I got there in five minutes. No more Road Runners. And no more hooded stunt drivers.

Joyce's apartment building was a study in wasted space. It had been built over thirty years ago, when the hustle for faster and easier dollars had been significantly lower. Morris Garden looked like a cross between a motel and an army barracks. It occupied nearly half a city block. The red brick structure was only one story high.

Narrow sidewalks branched out from the parking lot to the various entrances of the building. It was a 150-foot walk across a hilly lawn to the nearest entrance. More than a few moving van men, I am sure, had cursed it over the years. If Morris Garden were built today, it would be fourteen stories high and come equipped with an elevator that didn't work half the time. The parking lot would be miniaturized into a rectangle of macadam with the parking stalls so narrow that only the most compact cars would not violate the white dividing lines. Gone, too, would be the rolling lawn where tenants held summer night barbecues. In its place would be—what?—another high-rise apartment building, of course. Morris Garden II. Or Son of Morris Garden. Taller. Lower quality building materials. Higher rent.

"You sure you don't want anything?" Joyce asked.

"No, this coffee's fine. I'm not hungry. You go ahead."

She rustled around in her pantry, preparing a sandwich. I sat on a wooden rocking chair in her living room, resting a steaming mug on my lap. I heard a yelp and a hiss. A large white ball of fur barreled out from under the couch, followed by a smaller, gray ball.

"Chris and Star. Stop it," Joyce yelled.

The two cats skittered and slid around the living room floor with the energy of animated cartoon characters. They both lost steam at the same time. After catching his breath, each jumped up on a different window ledge to watch the rain and to rest up for another chase.

"Okay if I turn on the TV?"

"Sure."

I kept changing stations until I found a local channel. A newscast was beginning. Our hit-and-run had occurred too early in the morning to be included in today's *Dispatch*, and I was certain that it was not serious enough to merit a mention on the TV news.

"Anything interesting?" she said.

She was still busy in the pantry. What the hell kind of sandwich could take so long? A Bumstead special?

"Yeah. Something real interesting, as a matter of fact."

The clip had been taped at Niagara Falls. The scene was all too familiar. An escape artist, suspended upside down by a rope, struggled to free himself from a straitjacket. The

142

rope was afire, thus severely limiting his escape time. The rope was attached to a crane. Directly below him was the edge of the American Falls.

I sipped my coffee while patiently waiting for him to shed the straitjacket. I knew he would be successful. Had he failed, the story would have aired at the top of the broadcast, and his fatal trip down the falls would have been replayed in slow motion from three different angles.

After the magician triumphantly freed himself and the crane swung back, depositing him on safe ground, the reporters gathered around for interviews. As of yet, I had not heard a mention of the escape artist's name. I tried to guess who it was. The names of four prominent escapists sprang to mind. They were the only ones I knew that had the audacity to pull off the stunt. They were also the only ones with the expertise to manipulate the press into giving such grand coverage.

A tight close-up of the magician's face filled the screen. His blond, curly hair was drenched with water droplets and sweat. His smile was boyish, and I immediately sensed the charge of charisma emanating from him. He had the appeal of a national star, and he fielded questions from the press with the wit and ease of someone with twenty years' experience.

But he could not have had twenty years' experience. He was only nineteen, just out of high school.

I had never heard of him before.

Joyce came into the living room carrying the sandwich she had labored over.

"What are you watching?"

"The story of my life."

"Oh yeah? I didn't see it listed in *TV Guide.*"

"This biography is totally unauthorized. They're not even using my name. They're just stealing my script."

"Have a bite?"

"God, what is this? You worked all that time on this dinky thing?"

The sandwich was a dainty affair, made of lightly browned toast and containing a combination of lettuce, tomato, and an unknown green spread. It was sliced into four triangles that were impaled by toothpicks. It was prettier than a photo on a Howard Johnson's menu.

"No mention of our wreck?" she asked.

"No. What's this green stuff?"

"That's what took so long. It's a secret recipe. Mostly mayonnaise, with a lot of spices and chopped vegetables mixed in."

"Don't worry. Your secret is safe with me."

She nibbled while we watched the weather forecaster name areas of the country, and then point to all the wrong places on the color satellite map.

"Joyce. I'm done."

"With what?"

"This whole lousy case."

"Why give up? It's just starting to get dangerous."

"I'm not quitting. I'm just done. Through. Through putzing around, gingerly tiptoeing through the messes of other people's lives and trying not to stir things up. It's really not what I do best."

"What do you do best? Scratch that question. I know what you do best. What do you do second best?"

One of her cats sprang down from the windowsill and up onto my lap in one motion. It arched its back, prepping itself for a long snooze. I stroked it behind the ears. I wish I could make friends with people that easily.

"This one's Star?"

"Yes. Because she's so white."

"I'll tell you what I do best. Better yet. I'll show you. Just suspend me from a crane above Niagara Falls and watch me try to escape from a straitjacket. And be sure to have plenty of reporters on hand."

"I don't think we have any waterfalls near here. How about a dried-up reservoir?"

"Water's not necessary. Not to put on a show. The only things I need are an audience and a slate of entertainment. If I can ring up some long-distance bills on your phone, I can get started right away."

"Be my guest."

The anchorman was recapping the headlines. One of the stories was about a local man whose car was found in a wooded area. Apparently he had lost control and run off the road, caroming off several trees. He was D.O.A.

"Wasn't as lucky as us, was he?" Joyce said.

"Recognize his name? Dennis Rockwell?"

"No."

144

Joyce's cat was still nestled on my lap. Purring. Unconscious. Catatonic, in fact.

If I'm going to stir things up, I thought, I might as well start here. "Dennis Rockwell was the reference librarian we talked to today."

I suddenly straightened to a standing position. Joyce's cat yelped with shock at my disappearing lap. I had lost a friend as quickly as I had made one.

The first person I called was Sergeant Paul Fetterman.

CHAPTER TWENTY-FIVE

I hung up and promptly dialed the City Hall number that was jotted in my notebook. Fetterman's son had answered the home phone, sounding sad. He told me his father was out; he didn't know where. I asked him what was wrong. He told me that Daddy had burned himself again on the soldering iron, blaming it all on him. I told him that when his dad heard the beautiful music on the hi-fi or shortwave radio or whatever it was they were building, he would forget all about the little burn. The boy said he was not so sure. The bandage around Daddy's hand was very big.

The switchboard operator rang the phone on Fetterman's desk, and he answered after three rings.

"How's the hand?" I said.

"How—? Eddie told you? I was reading the instructions, and I asked him to hand me the soldering iron. I didn't look up. The poor kid put the business end in my hand. I'm not sure what scared him more: how loud I yelled or the words I used."

"Wish I could have been there. The reason I called is I want to know if you've checked out the description of that car."

"Christ, do you think I'm eating and sleeping this case? Don't you think I have other things to worry about?"

I didn't answer. After a long silence, he said, "Yeah, someone ran it down for me. You were right. There was a car matching the description of the one that ran you off the road. It was parked in the garage the night Morrow died. Its license number had some of the numbers you gave me. And—"

"—and it was a stolen vehicle, right?"

"Yeah. Stolen. It wasn't on any hot list until after Morrow's death. Hey, Colderwood, you don't need me, except maybe as a job reference. There's a vacant desk here beside mine. I could probably get you a position on the force. We're always looking for a few more assholes who think they know more than the police."

"Thanks, but no thanks. I already have a profession, and I'm itching to get back to it. About this stolen car, I'd wager that it's from out of town, probably from the other side of the state."

"That's right. Wilkes-Barre. Sounds like you've got some answers to this thing. Want to let me in on your secret?"

"I wish I had a few more answers. I do know of one man who had a lot more answers."

"His name?"

"Sorry. He's dead at the moment. And I'm not referring to Morrow. I'd like you to do one more thing, Sergeant."

"Yeah?"

"I'd like you to come to a magic show. I'll be in touch when I know the exact time and place. Take care of that hand, you hear?"

CHAPTER TWENTY-SIX

Joyce did not have an elegant, state-of-the-art telephone like Logan Zoller's. Hers was a simple, black desk model with a rotary dial. The coiled cord between the receiver and the base was so kinked it had shrunk to two feet. When I had an apartment, back in the days when it looked like I might be spending more than a month at a time in one city, I owned a push-button phone. I got off on the musical notes it made when I punched the buttons. I was able to wangle from the phone company a number that, when the buttons were pushed in order, matched the first seven notes of "In-A-Gadda-Da-Vida."

If I ever own another phone, I'll get the same number again. If you can figure out my number, give me a ring at three-thirty some morning. It won't wake me, though. Just my telephone message recorder, which does not like to be activated any more than I do at that hour.

There was no answer at Logan Zoller's house. Not even a sleepy answering machine. I tried the bookshop number. Zoller answered on the twelfth ring.

After I identified myself, he said, "I'm glad you called."

"Why's that?"

I listened closely for any trace of nervousness or strain. Or overfriendliness or overcasualness.

"I have good news about that book you wanted, *Greater Magic.* If you're still serious, I have a seller."

"Great. Who is it?"

"Sorry, that's confidential. If buyers and sellers get together on their own, they don't need me, do they?"

"I see."

"If you're interested, I need a deposit. In cash."

"Good. You'll be at the store for a while?"

148

"At least another hour."

"I'll drop by. See you."

I looked at my watch. There would be plenty of time.

"Can I come along?" Joyce asked.

"No. You don't want to be involved in a felony. To be exact, a B and E."

"What?"

"Breaking and entering."

"If I come along, maybe I can prevent a G.C."

"G.C.?"

"Getting caught."

"You're on."

CHAPTER TWENTY-SEVEN

Call it nerves.

Call it heightened sense of reality.

Call it being scared witless.

Call it what you want; Joyce and I chattered incessantly during our short drive.

We bandied back and forth unanswered questions about the Morrow case.

Who is Mrs. Morrow's lover?

Who ran us off the road?

Who tried to kill me in my motel room?

What was Zoller's connection with Jack Fireeno, the local racketeer?

What was the real reason for Dr. Randy Pescatore's presence at the police station the night of Morrow's death, the night Fetterman and his men hauled me in?

Neither of us had any answers. To each question, we responded with yet one more question. We both sensed that if we could find the key to just one puzzle, then all the solutions would slide into place.

However, since the pieces weren't dropping gracefully into place, I was now willing to jump with both feet on a piece or two.

We drove past Editions. It was the only shop on the street with lights still on. Zoller stood behind the counter, gazing at a book. His reading glasses sat at the tip of his nose. He turned the pages too fast for reading. Perhaps he was inspecting its condition. Perhaps he was scouring it for hundred-dollar bills he had squirreled away.

Either way, it did not matter. Zoller was still at the shop. Which meant he was not at home. Which meant I would not be rudely interrupted when I busted in.

My experience with locks had always been in breaking out, never in. And it was always in front of hundreds of people, never a solo performance. My only audience to-night was Joyce, but her real job was to keep an eye out for unexpected visitors. If I heard the horn toot twice, I would know that she was pulling away, that I was on my own and should get the hell out of there.

My heart pumped so fiercely it hurt. Zoller's back door lock was as challenging as untying an overhand knot is to a Cub Scout. Within seconds I was in his kitchen, smelling the aroma of the bacon he'd had for breakfast.

Although I didn't think I'd overstay my welcome, I hit the stopwatch button on my wristwatch. I was giving my-self no more than thirty minutes.

Not wanting to rush and get sloppy, I concentrated my search in the most likely area. If I came up empty-handed, I intended to pay a secret visit to the bookshop, too. I didn't relish the thought.

I searched Zoller's basement workshop first. Once down-stairs, I switched off my penlight. There were no windows, so I turned on all the lights, knowing I wouldn't be adver-tising my presence. I had grossly underestimated the time needed for a thorough search. I spent almost thirty min-utes alone in his workshop. If Joyce had lain on the car horn, I'm not sure I would have heard.

I found it in a footlocker beneath Zoller's workbench. He had assembled a nifty kit: cotton swabs, ten varieties of rubber erasers, magnets, and over thirty shades of creamy Meltonian shoe polish. I replaced everything as I had found it. My discovery made my actions feel less criminal.

No degree of stealth decreased my noise in exiting. Everything creaked and groaned. The cellar stairs, the kitchen floor, even my bones. In the kitchen, my penlight dropped to the kitchen floor like a lightning bolt. In retrieving it, I tripped over a kitchen chair. As I headed through the backyard, my mind played wicked tricks on me. Did I turn off the basement lights? I couldn't remem-ber.

Tough.

I was not going back in. Not for a pot of gold or a cache of rare papers once owned by Houdini. Let Zoller wonder if he had left the light on in his workshop, which I bet he had visited not too many hours ago.

"Get what you wanted?" Joyce asked.

"Start the car up. Let's go. Yeah. I did. Turn here. Not too fast."

"Do you have it on you?"

"No, I left everything there."

"What were you looking for?"

"The Rosetta stone."

"Anything else?"

"Leakey's Missing Link."

"How's that?"

"Let's just say we won't be jumping on any more puzzle pieces."

"Was it hot in there? You need a shower. You're wet."

"First we have a magic book to pick up. By the way, did you turn out the kitchen light in your apartment?"

"No. Yes. Oh, I don't remember."

"Good. Maybe Zoller won't remember about his basement light."

CHAPTER TWENTY-EIGHT

When we arrived at Editions, Zoller was all business. I was happy to give him his deposit for the magic book and get out quickly.

We intended to head back to Joyce's apartment, but the memory of a shininess on the front door of the bookstore nagged at me. I decided to make one more stop. I was glad Mrs. Morrow was at home.

"I still don't understand," Joyce said as Mrs. Morrow made her way down the hallway from the study to her living room where Joyce and I waited. "Why do you need the bookstore keys? You didn't need keys to get into Zoller's house. Won't this make you look suspicious if he later reports the store burglarized?"

"I don't intend to burgle. Just *attempt.*"

Mrs. Morrow dangled the keys in front of her as she walked into the room.

"Fine. Thank you," I said as she laid them on the coffee table.

I withdrew from my pocket the handful of keys that I had removed from Joyce's and my key cases. I spread them on the coffee table and painstakingly compared each one with those on the bunch that Mrs. Morrow had brought me. She did not notice me slip off and palm the one stamped E.B.S.

"Find anything?" Mrs. Morrow asked when I returned the keys to her.

"Not what I hoped, but it was worth a try."

She did not ask why I examined the keys, so I did not have to tell her any lies.

"Are you making progress in your investigation, Mr. Colderwood?"

"Not as fast as I'd like. I was going to call you tonight, Mrs. Morrow, but since I'm here, I'll make an unusual request."

I outlined my plan, giving as little detail as necessary. Although she was mildly confused, I was persuasive enough that, after initial hesitation and objection, she finally said yes.

"I'll get back to you tonight with the exact times, as soon as I set things up with the others. I apologize for not being more explicit, but I will be able to give you more information tomorrow."

"If you think it will clear up the questions surrounding Dean's death, by all means go ahead with this thing."

"If Professor Gastini won't cooperate, I'll have to rig things myself. I'm far from an expert in his area, so that's why I need an extra two thousand dollars to hire Gastini. I know he won't take less. When he comes—*if* he comes—please follow his instructions to the letter."

Joyce and I rose to leave.

"One more thing, Mrs. Morrow. Have you held anything back?"

"No. I haven't lied."

"Mrs. Morrow, I know you've lied. You've got your reasons, I'm sure. But I'm afraid they can't outweigh the two attempts on my life so far."

"Two?"

"Yes. First there was the beating in my motel room. And then this morning someone quite persuasively urged Joyce and me to make a new roadway out of a ditch along Le-Boeuf Road. Her car is in the back lot of an auto body shop now, awaiting the learned eye of the insurance adjuster."

Mrs. Morrow nervously toyed with the ring of keys. I hoped she didn't notice that it was one key light. For a moment, but only for a moment, I thought she was going to tell us everything.

"Mr. Colderwood. You knew there were elements of danger when I hired you. I did not authorize your subcontracting some of the responsibilities to Miss Gildea. I am sorry about your close scrapes. But, as they say, that's all part of the game."

"Miss Gildea has her own interests in this situation, Mrs. Morrow. She is accepting no money. You never instructed me as to how to conduct my research into your husband's dealings. You didn't say I couldn't take on a partner. You tossed the money my way and sat back here in your palace waiting for my results.

"Don't get me wrong. I'm very pleased that you are going along with my scheme for day after tomorrow. But just remember, before you turn in tonight—if you think you can get any sleep—I am bringing a pretty unsavory crew into your house. Just as you can't guarantee what happens to me out there on the streets, I can't guarantee what's going to happen here in your house. This little drama I'm throwing together has an unscripted ending. The more I know before the curtain rises, the safer you'll be. Because day after tomorrow, Mrs. Morrow, those streets out there are coming home."

The keys jingled faster in her hands, but she said nothing more. She blinked back tears I knew would be flowing freely after Joyce and I left. They were tears of fear. Tears of the truly alone.

"You've got Joyce's number. If you decide to level with us, call any time. Joyce will probably answer. I'm going to be busy. I doubt if I get much sleep."

Joyce and I showed ourselves out, leaving Mrs. Morrow silently fretting in her living room. The same living room that soon would become a theatre. I hoped it wouldn't be a theatre of the absurd.

CHAPTER TWENTY-NINE

Our approach to the bookshop was less subtle than it was to Logan Zoller's house. We avoided any sort of furtive actions.

Joyce parked a foot away from the curb in front of the shop and left the engine running. I slammed the door behind me and strolled up to the entrance, key in hand, as if I owned the place. This mission was a lot simpler than the previous one that night, so nerves were not a problem.

Zoller had pasted a small red and gold decal on the front door glass of the shop. The letters were luminous, presumably visible in even the dimmest light. They proclaimed that this business was now protected by the Black Knight Security System. The sign had not been on the door when I had stood outside it a couple of days ago. The warning did not exactly make me shake in my boots, let alone in my wing tips.

I wondered if Zoller had simply bought himself a couple of cheap sound-activated burglar alarms or if he had gone all out and installed a system that, at the slightest violation, would light up a Christmas tree in City Hall and dispatch a regiment of cops, replete with megaphones, shotguns, and hungry German shepherds. If it did, I did not intend to be around to find out.

I slipped the key into the lock. It was the one marked E.B.S., which I had lifted from Mrs. Morrow's key ring. It refused to turn the lock. After much jiggling and doorknob shaking, I gave up.

I did not hear any alarm sound after the jolting I had given the door. Perhaps Zoller's sole investment in beefed-up security was a thirty-cent Black Knight Security decal and a changed lock. Of course, maybe the alarm was a silent one, sending a secret signal to police head-quarters. I was back in the car in a few seconds.

"Were you right?"

"Yeah, I was right."

Joyce put the car in gear, and we tooled down the street faster than any Black Knight could ever hope to pursue us.

My appetite had returned. I could not identify from aroma alone what Joyce had sizzling and hissing in a frying pan in her kitchen, but I felt my stomach rumble in delight at the thought of a full meal. I finished dialing the number, and the telephone made its usual pattern of clicks and hums before it rang at the other end. After three rings someone answered.

"Hello. Aldo Gastini speaking."

I could never get over the fact that he had not been born in an English-speaking country. Through assiduous drilling, he had eliminated all trace of accent from his speech. His voice, which would have been the envy of any 1940s radio show narrator, still radiated the warmth and resonance that was his trademark. If I didn't know the truth, I would never have guessed from his voice that Gastini was well into his seventies.

"This is Harry Colderwood, Aldo. Here's a quick question for you. Are you still working?"

"Perhaps I should ask you the same question "

"Oh, don't worry about me. I am working very hard, inching my way down from stardom to total obscurity. Unlike you, I didn't take the plunge all at once."

"Harrumph," he harrumphed. "You must be making some kind of big bucks to pay for a call like this. You're still out in L.A., aren't you?"

"No, that was two jobs ago. And I'm not really paying for this call. As a matter of fact, I'm not all that far away. Two hundred miles at the most."

"Great. We'll have to get together. So you really think I was a star? Come on, Harry. In the most detailed book ever written on the history of magic, I will never rate more than a footnote. You, sir, will have a whole chapter devoted to you. It will be titled 'Famous Fuck-Ups in Magic.' "

"There might be some room in that chapter for you, Aldo. I've always maintained that what you've been trying to do is tantamount to producing a big-budget silent picture twenty years after talkies came in."

"You're totally wrong, Harry. If I have any judgment in public taste at all, I'd say that the time is ripe now for a revival of the traveling spook show."

"Sure. Right after the Glenn Miller and Tommy Dorsey orchestras recapture the top ten."

I had read enough of his articles and interviews in magic magazines to know his arguments thoroughly. Sometimes his logic even begins to make sense. Maybe the country's insatiable lust for horror and supernatural will soften enough to create a demand for the kind of delightfully eerie entertainment that Gastini had brought us decades before. Yet, I had trouble imagining the same youngsters who were crowding the theatres to see *The Mutilation of Brownie Troop No. 666* also being moved to the edge of their seats by the pixilations of the little floating goblins and tap-dancing skeletons that were the highlight of Aldo Gastini's spook show.

"Tell you what, Harry. When one of the big movie theatre chains signs me to a lengthy contract, I'll be sure to dedicate the first show to you. No, I'll do better than that. If you're still out of work, I'll give you a job—loading and unloading our trucks.

"Is this a business or social call, Harry? No, I'll answer that myself. It's a business, isn't it? When it came to other magicians, you never did fraternize much."

"You're a fine one to talk, Great Gastini. When I was a kid, I couldn't wait for my next copy of *Genii* magazine to see who you were going to skewer next in your column."

"That was show biz, son. I never meant any harm. Just good, clean, vicious fun, and it kept punks like you coming back to the magazine every month for more."

"If it's business you want, then it's business you'll get, Aldo. Straightforward and to the point. How much do you charge for a show?"

"What kind of show?"

"Christ, Aldo, I'm not calling you to do a kid's birthday party. What kind of show do you do best?"

"I've never done just one spook show before. I usually book an entire tour."

"I just love it when people refer to something they haven't done in twenty-five years as 'usually.' Come on, Aldo, how much?"

"Let me think."

I imagined the clicks and pops on the phone line to be the rusty, creaky wheels turning in the financial section of Gastini's head.

"What's there to think about?" I said. "Do you have a crew? Any assistants to pay?"

"I did have one young kid. He's been gone for over a year now. After working side by side with me for a year, he just came to me one day and said that he was tired of being a protégé to a buggy-whip maker. That's what he called me. A buggy-whip maker. He said the spook show business was one big joke."

"So you will need some help."

"Mostly in setting up. My granddaughters help with the actual production. I can operate everything once it's in place. How big a theatre are we talking about?"

"I'm not hiring you for a theatre, Aldo. This is going to be done in someone's living room. It's a big living room, though."

"Living room? My show's designed to be done in halls that hold at least seven hundred people."

"This living room's not quite that big. Would two thousand dollars be enough money?"

Joyce set up a metal TV tray in front of me. She left the room and returned with a steaming dish of vegetables and what looked like bits of chicken. I looked at her questioningly.

"It's chicken Peking. I'll bring the fried rice in a minute," she whispered.

I could almost feel Gastini weighing the situation, trying to decide if this would be the easiest or the hardest two thousand dollars he ever made. Even though it was Mrs. Morrow's money that I was bargaining with, I still did not want to waste any of it.

"Let me fill you in on exactly what I want, Aldo."

"Yes, do that. Good Jesus, I can't believe it. I'm reduced to playing living rooms. Only one step away from playing toilets. Go ahead. I'm listening."

159

I started to explain, but Gastini interrupted and told me to hold on while he got a pencil and paper. I heard him muttering in the background.

"Living rooms. I'm playing goddam living rooms," he said.

CHAPTER THIRTY

Even after being heaped with a third helping of chicken Peking, my plate lay empty atop the TV tray, scraped clean, leaving only a thin layer of gravy. Next to it stood the tall glass I had been sipping from for the last couple of hours. Three inches of light gold liquid sat at the bottom, a result of three neglected ice cubes. The pile of butts in the ashtray was a molehill slowly working its way up to mountaindom.

No more cigarettes. No more tonight, I promised myself. My lungs felt dried out, and I sensed an impending coughing jag.

Joyce was curled up beside me on the couch. Her breathing was regular, but her sleep looked uncomfortable. When had she changed into that nightgown? I reached over and stroked her, from her shoulder down to the curve of her hip. She didn't stir.

God, how many calls have I made tonight?

I looked at the list. Almost a whole page. There was a check mark beside each name that I had called. I was too tired to count the checks.

I fired up another cigarette. Last one. Last one tonight. I promise.

How many calls did I have left to make? One. No, two if you count *that* one. Well, I would have to decide later if I was going to make that last one.

I didn't want to wait until tomorrow morning. I knew I had a better chance of catching everyone at home at night. The later it got, the more I felt like a damned telephone solicitor. Was it my imagination, or was a black ring beginning to form around my dialing finger?

I dialed *that* number, not being able to put it off any longer. I made sure I got the area code right. No use getting someone from the wrong part of the country out of bed. I hoped I was sharp enough to handle the delicate nature of the call.

"Hello. Fryer's. Peter speaking."

"Mr. Fryer. My name is Harry Colderwood. I—"

The sleep instantly disappeared from the man's voice.

"The magician?" he said.

"Yes. That's me. I'm calling about your son."

"Yes?" There was expectation in his voice. I hated to deflate it.

"I'd like to speak with him, if I could."

"Oh," he said, communicating his crushed hope in just one word.

He started talking with someone else. With his hand over the phone, it sounded as if I had a funnel against my ear. I could not understand what he was saying.

"Mr. Colderwood. Sorry for the interruption. We've—my wife and I—have been very anxious about our son. Do you have any word on him?"

"I'm afraid not, Mr. Fryer. Is there something wrong with your son?"

"We haven't heard from Peter, Jr., for several months now. The police have done absolutely nothing, except to tell us not to worry. We haven't taken their advice. We're worried."

"To be perfectly honest with you, Mr. Fryer, I am not sure I can be of assistance to you. But there is a slim chance I can help if you'll let me ask a few questions. How old is Peter, Jr.?"

"He's—how old is Peter, honey? He's twenty-four, Mr. Colderwood."

In answer to my questions, he told me that Peter had graduated from the Capitol Campus of Penn State, had never gotten a full-time job, and had lived off and on at home until three months ago. That's when he took off.

"Mr. Fryer, when I gave you my name, you knew who I was right away, and you didn't seem to surprised that I'd be calling you. Why?"

"We frequently got calls from magicians from all over the country. They were mostly the ones that Peter read about in his magic magazines, but we'd hear sometimes from the famous ones that we saw on television. Peter cor-

162

responded with them all. He was totally immersed in magic."

I promised myself to look through my letters when I got back to New Jersey, to see if there were any from a Peter Fryer. I did not recall the name.

"Peter wanted to be just like you, Mr. Colderwood. A professional magician."

Mr. Fryer estimated that the driving time from Bayorvale to his home was less than three hours. I made an appointment to visit him tomorrow. He was anxious to try anything to learn his son's whereabouts. I cautioned him about being overly optimistic.

There was one more call that I wanted to make, and I had to nag myself to make it. I picked up the phone again and dialed. In the middle of the second ring, someone answered.

"Hello." Her voice was timid. Barely audible.

"Doctor Randolph Pescatore, please," I said.

The line went dead with a click. Just as I expected.

CHAPTER THIRTY-ONE

I awoke in the midst of a nightmare that forced me to relive the sideswiping incident of the day before—except that this time pain and injury paid me a nasty visit. A permanent one.

My eyes flew open, and I dropped the *Genii* magazine I had been reading before I nodded off. I was halfway across the room before I realized where I was: Joyce's living room. The wall clock said 4:58 A.M.

Joyce's two cats had been asleep at my feet but had scattered when the magazine slapped onto the floor between them. They were in self-exile underneath or behind some furniture.

Joyce was no longer sleeping on the sofa. I peeked in her bedroom and saw that she was sprawled facedown on her bed. She had not even removed the bedspread. In her sleep, she had assumed a posture to make a chiropractor wince. I padded softly through the apartment, trying not to awaken her.

I took a shower that was too hot. I threw on so much aftershave that my face was numb with the sting. When I made my morning coffee, I threw in two scoops of instant instead of one. I drank it as fast as I could. Then I made another, this time making it even blacker. It was all an attempt to shock my system out of its yearning for more sleep. It did not work very well. The only solution now for my nagging fatigue was three solid days of ten-hour snoozes.

I found some typing paper in a desk in the living room. I started to write Joyce a note explaining what I was going to do today. When I saw how long it would take to put everything on paper, I reluctantly woke her up. I was running late, so I talked fast.

I told her of my late-night conversation with Peter Fryer, Sr. I also gave her the best advice I could on how to handle the eccentric, sometimes almost aberrant, behavior of Aldo Gastini. I then gave her the best estimate I could as to when I would return. Late afternoon. Maybe early evening.

Armed with yet another cup of strong coffee, I left the apartment to begin my journey halfway across the state.

Fryer's directions were accurate. Making no wrong turns and not having to backtrack once, I arrived at his home in Clarks Summit a half hour ahead of schedule. The Fryers lived in a one-story rancher at the end of a dead-end street. Their house was nearly hidden from view by a high but meticulously trimmed hedge that ran the length of their lawn and was interrupted only by their driveway.

Fryer must have been waiting for me by a window. The front door was open, and he was out in the driveway to greet me before I even had a chance to shut off the engine of the Chevette.

His handshake was overly firm, and his smile only accentuated the newly etched lines on his face. He was a man carrying a burden that he desperately wanted to be rid of.

"How was your trip? My directions all right? Could you use a snack? I mean, have you had your lunch yet?"

"What's that? Oh, no, thank you. I'm fine."

"What are you looking at? What—?"

He turned around and saw who I had been staring at. Framed in the small square window of his front door was a woman's face. I could not immediately tell how old she was. Her hair was either very light, or gray had begun to conquer it prematurely. Her stare was passive and unrelenting.

"Oh. That's my wife. She's curious about your call last night, too. Why don't you come in and meet her."

I waded through their questions as quickly as I could and asked to see a picture of their son. His framed graduation picture was set atop the piano in their living room.

I immediately recognized Peter Fryer, Jr.

That had been the real purpose of my journey. To see his picture. To confirm my suspicions.

Or had I driven several hundred miles for something else? I could have arranged to have his parents send a snapshot by express courier while I sat tight in Bayorvale. Why else had I made the drive?

"I'd like to see Peter's room."

"Of course," his mother said.

Mrs. Fryer was a woman who looked as if she had reached the age of forty and decided to skip the next decade. She carried the oppression of constant guilt and worry even less well than her husband. Her walk was listless as I followed her to her son's bedroom.

Peter Fryer, Jr.'s bedroom was a mini-museum of magic. In much the same way that many young American males' rooms were shrines to sports, Peter had on display a dazzling array of magic posters, pictures, relics, and apparatus. Some of the posters and equipment were originals and quite valuable.

A small, highly polished wooden chest with a lock on the front sat on a shelf. Beside it was a huge key that fit the lock. Closer examination confirmed my suspicions.

"This was made by Sam Lloyd. It's a prediction chest. Mentalists use them to predict headlines weeks before they are actually published in the newpaper. Lloyd produced a limited number of them; each one was numbered. When new, it cost two hundred dollars. It could easily bring over a thousand dollars now."

"Up until last year, Peter was doing quite well at booking shows in the area," Mrs. Fryer said. "Except for an occasional birthday or Christmas gift from us, he paid for all the equipment in his show and everything you see on display here."

"Reminds me of my bedroom when I was growing up," I said.

His posters and publicity photos featured performers who were known to the general public, like Blackstone, Houdini, Mark Wilson, and Dunninger. He also had on display pictures of magicians who were celebrities mostly within the magic community itself, like Ted Annemann, Jean Hugard, and Dr. Harlan Tarbell. Oh, yes, he had an early publicity still of me. In the picture, I stood in an awkward pose wearing slicked-back hair, a rented tux that was a size too big, and a top hat that refused to stay on straight. A dove was perched on my finger. Its wings were spread, and it looked like a miniature white eagle. I was not sure which category young Peter included me in—the celebrity magicians or the magicians' magicians. Probably a little of both.

"Your husband said that Peter corresponded a lot."

"He kept his letters there. Go through them if you want."

She pointed to a file drawer in his desk. I pulled it open. It was jammed with letters. He had a folder for each magician that he had written to: Dai Vernon, Sigfried and Roy, Tom Ogden, and dozens of others. There was also a file labeled "Colderwood, Harry." I pulled it out and saw that I had written to Peter on three separate occasions six years ago. I could not recall the letters, but that didn't surprise me. Sometimes I wrote so many letters that they all became a blur.

Based on my replies, it appeared that Peter was attempting to learn a complicated move from a cut and restored rope routine of mine. I had sympathized with Peter's problems and I had written a paragraph of clarification, even including a sketch indicating where his fingers should be during each of the crucial steps of the move.

Another letter of mine was a perfunctory thank-you for a letter of congratulations Peter had sent me after a successful talk show appearance.

Just like his poster and picture gallery, Peter's letter file was a who's who of magic of the last decade. There were even two letters from Aldo Gastini, which greatly surprised me. I knew Gastini would rather talk for an hour long-distance than sit down and write. Letter by letter, I thumbed my way through his correspondence. Mrs. Fryer left me alone, hoping that I could uncover something they were unable to. My journey through the letters was wistful, enabling me to forget the events of the past several days.

When I finished, I closed the desk drawer and sat back in the chair. What did I expect to find? A letter from L. Dean Morrow? A note from Peter that began, "Dear Mr. Colderwood: This is where I am and what happened . . ."?

Peter, like most conjurers I know, allowed some wall space for an "action" picture of himself. I removed it from the wall and propped it up on the desk in front of me. Unlike most publicity shots of amateur magicians, in which they attempt to crowd in every piece of glittering, chintzy equipment they can, Peter's picture was quite simple.

He wore a plain three-piece suit and sat on a stool. He had his eyes closed, and he held a white, sealed envelope to his forehead in an attempt to "read" the contents. The caption below the photograph indicated that he was performing a version of a mentalist effect that was now considered by many to be in bad taste. In that effect, the audience would write on slips of paper the names of relatives, some who were still living, and others who were now deceased. The slips would be sealed in envelopes, and the mentalist's job was to divine whether each envelope contained the name of a living or dead person.

It was an anachronism to see a young, modern magician performing this ghoulish and outdated trick. I had trouble believing that Peter Fryer could seriously include this effect in a magic act that was obviously successful enough to buy the expensive props and posters on display in the room.

I sat for a few more minutes studying the picture of Peter, whose face was almost completely dark under the shadow of the envelope that he was attempting to read. The words printed below the photo took on a different meaning for me, as I am sure they did for his parents. The caption said: "LIVING OR DEAD?" "You got me, Peter," I said to myself. "Are you or aren't you?"

I sneezed twice because of the dust I had stirred up from flipping through the letter file. I replaced the picture on the wall, taking care to straighten it precisely. I could imagine Mrs. Fryer making daily visits to the bedroom, dusting things that didn't need dusting and straightening things that didn't need straightening. I wondered if the Fasicks in Somerset had done the same with Lou's bedroom while awaiting her return.

Maybe Mrs. Fryer found comfort in the ritual, but her husband clearly did not. He would not even come into the bedroom when she was showing it to me.

I lingered there, not wanting to return to the living room and have the conversation I knew I was going to have with them. I felt at home in Peter's bedroom, more than I had anywhere else in the last few days. I remembered my own teenage days, going to bed surrounded by scores of photos of the great wonder workers of the world. It was hard to sleep sometimes; I was so obsessed with the thought of someday joining the gallery of conjurers that lined my walls. I achieved that goal—for a while, anyway.

It was cruel to make the Fryers wait, knowing that they had so many unanswered questions. But there was one big question I would have to ask them first. I walked back into the living room, where they were silently waiting for me.

"Before I tell you how I found out about Peter and all that has happened to lead me here, I must ask you to be perfectly frank. I'm not even sure how to ask you this. But would you please tell me about Peter—from the beginning."

"From when he disappeared?" Mr. Fryer asked.

"No. I mean from the *very* beginning. You both know, I'm sure, what I'm talking about."

Mr. Fryer cleared his throat, but it was his wife who began talking. I settled back in the couch to listen, wishing the hell I was back in Peter's bedroom, playing with his magic toys.

CHAPTER THIRTY-TWO

Aided by a strong tail wind and a determination not to be late for my other appointment, I made it back to Bayorvale in less than three hours. I kept the windows down the whole way back. The November chill that filled the car did nothing to temper the guilt I felt about the false hopes I may have instilled in the Fryers. But at least it kept me awake.

By the time I pulled into the parking lot of the Bayorvale Public Library, I was sneezing quite regularly. The inside of my nose had been invaded by a painful tickle. The process of refrigerating the interior of the car must have given undue encouragement to some cold germs swimming around inside me.

Inside the library, I asked the lady at the main desk where the administrative director's office was. I followed her directions, which took me downstairs and through a series of doors. I made many left and right turns. The boiler room would have been easier to find. I finally found a door with the name Willard Hollen on it. The name was written on a file card with a Flair pen. It was taped to the door. Four other names were written above Hollen's. Each had a thick line drawn through it. The door next to Hollen's office said "Furnace Room."

I knocked, but no one answered. I knocked again, and when there was no response, I rapped a few times on the furnace room door for good measure. No luck there either. Since I was exactly on time for my appointment, I walked into his office without knocking again.

There was no secretary inside, just a man watching TV. He had his back to me, and he was wearing a set of headphones. So, that's why he didn't answer. Silent light bolts zipped across the television screen, followed by starbursts and yellow and blue flashes. At first I thought it was a video game, but then two familiar faces filled the screen. William Shatner and the guy with the big ears.

I hated to interrupt his show, but I leaned over his desk and lightly tapped his shoulder, expecting to startle him. He simply turned to see who it was, sighed, reached over to a machine atop the TV, and hit a button. The screen went white. He had been watching a video tape.

He removed his headset and swiveled around to face me. "Can I help you?"

His windowpane plaid sport coat consisted of thin yellow lines on a blue-green background. He wore his lavender pinstripe shirt open at the neck, exposing a nest of gray chest hair. His hair was dark brown and dyed. A uniform network of curls sprouted all over his head. He looked like Harpo Marx playing insurance salesman.

"Willard Hollen? I'm Harry Colderwood."

"Colderwood. Colderwood," he said in a mutter. He aimlessly moved papers back and forth on his desk, pausing every now and then to look at a page. When he finished, the papers were in the same place as when he had started—an elaborate version of the magician's false shuffle.

"I made an appointment for three-thirty. It's now three thirty-five. I'm not interrupting anything important, am I?"

"No. No. You see, we have an audiovisual section in the library now. You can actually borrow films, audio tapes, and video cassettes from here. We like to make sure that each new tape is of good quality. Reviewing them is an absolute necessity."

"It's a dirty job, but someone has to do it, aye Captain?"

"Er, yeah."

He was lucky my phaser was only set on "Stun."

"I'm glad I could get in to see you today," I said. "This place seems to be closed more often than not."

"Reaganomics. Recession. Depression. Unemployment. Decreasing population. We could spend hours analyzing all the reasons. Everything's ganged up on us, and we're in the most severe budget crunch in the history of our system."

"Yes, I know. I already talked about it with one of your employees. Dennis Rockwell."

171

Hollen grew solemn.

"Oh. Dennis. You knew him? Good worker. Superb worker. We're going to miss him. A tragic accident."

"He wasn't a friend of mine. I only met him the other day. What I really wanted to talk to you about was his job here."

"Which one? He handled an amazing array of jobs here."

"So he said. Your interlibrary loan system is what I'm interested in."

"What about it?"

"I'd like to know if there's a way of tapping into your computer to get a readout on all the requests that Rockwell made in, say, the last six months. I would also like to know what books he simply requested availability information on, but did not borrow."

"That can't be done."

"Now, how the hell do you know? You didn't even stop to think it over. What do you say you and I and whoever you're training for Rockwell's position take a stroll over to where you keep your computer terminal? It probably wouldn't take much fiddling around to figure out how to get the information I want."

"I'm sorry. Everyone's on a tight schedule here, with people taking time off to go to Dennis's viewing. If that delays your research project, that's too bad. No concern of mine."

Research project? Was that what I told him I was working on when I called yesterday? I had forgotten.

I swiftly switched my phaser from "Stun" to "Kill."

"I see. Well, that's that, I guess. Just put your tape back on. I'll stay and watch. I don't even need any sound, so you can still wear your headphones. I don't even need popcorn."

He silently studied me for a while, trying to figure out how best to dispose of me. I pulled a chair up close to his desk and sat down, my arms folded across my chest.

After scratching his jaw with the nail of his thumb for a few moments, he made a quick grab for his phone and rapidly punched in a three-digit number. Did he think I was going to wrestle it from his hand?

"Maggie? This is Willard. Is Rich there? Well, find him and send him down to my office immediately. Emergency? How the hell should I know? Just get him down here."

172

He hung up the phone, keeping a wary eye on me.

"Is Rich your security man?"

He gave me a short, clipped nod.

"You'll probably call him back in a minute to tell him to forget about coming down."

"Like hell I will."

"Sure you will. You know, that video tape you were watching was fascinating."

"Why?" he said, suddenly growing suspicious.

"Mr. Hollen, I'm not a big fan of *Star Trek*. I've only watched a few episodes, but I do know the difference between cheaper TV special effects and the special effects of big-budget movies. Those exploding spaceships I saw on the screen were definitely from a movie, not TV. Funny thing, though. I've seen all the *Star Trek* flicks. I don't remember that scene from any of them. Is that, by any chance, one of those video tapes that movie companies issue with additional footage that was excluded from the theatrical release?"

"Yes, you're right. This tape included outtakes," he said, too quickly.

"That's one possibility. *Or,* it could be that that cassette is a copy of *Star Trek IV*, which is not due for release for at least a couple of weeks. Which is it?"

He tried to talk, but he had to preface it with a nervous chuckle.

"What would I be doing with something like that?"

"Probably nothing other than watching it for your own personal enjoyment and/or curiosity. The real question is what your employees in the A.V. section are doing with the tape. Offhand, I'd guess that they are running off copies to sell or rent. Sometimes, for popular movies, the prints are stolen and copied months before the pictures are released. I'm sure you have sophisticated enough equipment here to run a bootleg operation. Since crowds are going to be busting down theatre doors to see the new *Star Trek* movie, your boys in A.V. should be able to pull in quite a few dollars. It would certainly be a lot more than the flimsy salaries they're pulling in here. Am I right or am I wrong?"

His only answer was to drum his fingers in rapid contemplation.

"I'm not saying you're actually involved in the bootlegging. But you are certainly aware of it and have looked the other way. Joyce Gildea is a good friend of mine. Recognize her by-line? A story about video piracy probably wouldn't make it to the front page of the *Dispatch*. But use of public money by a public servant for such an operation would make a nice feature. When this story breaks, it's a sure bet there'll be yet one more name added to the card taped on your office door. The statewide news wires will surely pick up the story. And the FBI will definitely take an active interest. Now, how about—"

He was already on the phone.

"Maggie?" he said. "Did you find Rich yet? No? Good. Just forget about it. We don't need him. We could use your help, though. You've operated the teletype hookup for interlibrary loan before, haven't you? Great. How about taking a stroll over to Dennis's old office. There will be a gentleman there to meet you. Cooperate with him and give him any information he needs. Thanks."

He let out a long breath of air through puffed cheeks as he hung up the phone.

"If you'll excuse me . . . ," he said, picking up the headphones.

"Thanks."

"No story?"

"Not a word to anyone."

He swiveled his chair until his back was to me again. He replaced his headphones, and in a moment the screen was again lit up with the likeness of Kirk of the *Enterprise*. I left his office and began my search for an office with Rockwell's name on it. I felt as though I was nearing the end of my own five-year mission.

CHAPTER THIRTY-THREE

A bell tinkled, and the turnstile I was passing through went rigid. I jiggled it a few times, but it was locked.

"Sir?" the librarian said as she marched up to me. She was only slightly taller than five feet, and she had to tilt her head back to look me in the eye. But she conducted herself with confidence and authority of someone with years of dealing with bell-ringers.

"I'm locked in," I said. "Don't have to pay to leave your library, do I?"

I smiled. She did not.

"Sir. Have you checked out all the books you have with you?"

"I don't have any books. I don't even have a card."

"You didn't accidentally place any library items in your coat pockets? Every book we have here has a thin metal strip that is magnetized. When a book is checked out, we demagnetize it. Our machine in front of the turnstile will detect any books that still have a magnetic charge. Anyone trying to sneak out with unchecked books will be met with a locked turnstile. As you were. Sir, *do* you have any books inside your coat?"

"Absolutely not. Perhaps this set it off."

I pulled my key chain out of my pocket. It had a little toy compass attached to it.

"See? Magnetic. It might have tripped off your machine."

"Hardly," she said.

"Then you'll have to search me."

"Oh, I won't. We have a security man who takes care of that. If you'll kindly wait here, I'll page him."

My presence in their library was giving the security man quite a workout today.

"This is the only exit from this building," she said. "There are fire exits all around the library, but an alarm will sound if you try to open any of them."

She walked backwards, keeping her eyes on me, until she got to her desk. She picked up her phone.

I pulled a handkerchief out of my pocket and showed it on both sides. I held it loosely between my hands, and it suddenly went rigid. I whisked away the hank to reveal a thin, hardbound book.

"Now where did this come from?" I said. "While it was invisible and floating around in the air, it must have set off the alarm."

I placed it on her desk. She smiled triumphantly.

"Maybe I'll get a card here someday. This book looks good. I'd like to take up the hobby sometime."

It was a children's book entitled *Fun with Magic*.

The turnstile was still locked, so I backpedaled a couple of steps to get a running start. Maybe I started off on the wrong foot. Perhaps I did not give myself enough of a runway. Whatever the reason, when my toe caught on the turnstile, my slick leap was instantly transformed into a Ringling Brothers clown pratfall.

I tucked my head in and went into a ragged somersault as I slammed down onto the carpeted foyer of the library. I must have stumbled across the electric eye that controlled the entrance door. Lucky me. Otherwise I would have spent a long time picking glass shards out of myself. The huge glass door swung open in time for me to complete my acrobatic spin. When my feet slapped the ground again, I bounced to a complete standing position on the sidewalk outside the library. The door hissed closed behind me.

Four elementary school-age kids burst into applause. I thanked them and took a low bow, partly to clear the spinning from my head and partly because, well, because entertainment is my life.

The sign on Editions Bookshop said "Closed," but Logan Zoller was still doing business. I parked across the street from the shop and had a clear view of Zoller and another man talking. The transaction was uncomplicated. Zoller came out from the back room holding a book on his outstretched palms as carefully as if it were a tray full of drinks. The little man with the porkpie hat took the book, treating it with even more love than Zoller. He took several minutes to examine it. He even pulled a magnifying glass out of his coat pocket and gave it a thorough inspection.

Finally the man put away his magnifier and hinged the book closed again. He nudged back his hat from his forehead, and I barely perceived his nod of assent. The expressions on their faces were not so subtle. They had a duel to see who could manage the greediest smile.

The man handed Zoller a white envelope. Zoller slid out a stack of money from it. It would have been a sizable amount even if they were all one-dollar bills. I was sure they were not. Zoller counted them slowly and methodically. When he was done, Zoller said something, winked at the man, and pocketed the envelope of money.

The man slid his hat back down to his eyebrows and lifted it again in a good-bye tip. Zoller raised his hand in an intended handshake. He changed his mind and just gave a friendly wave. Zoller turned out the lights of the shop as soon as the man closed the front door behind him.

The man drove away in a late-model Lincoln that was parked in front of the store. It had Massachusetts plates. I tailed him and was not the least bit sneaky about it.

CHAPTER THIRTY-FOUR

Sometimes I can literally walk away from stage fright. That is, if I relentlessly pace back and forth enough, I can eventually lull myself into a state of relaxation. But not tonight.

L. Dean Morrow's study was too tiny to pace in. I contented myself with alternately standing up and sitting down whenever I felt the familiar invasion of butterflies. I was playing a one-man game of musical chairs.

It was eight o'clock, and everyone should have arrived by now. From the sound of clinking ice in glasses and the smell of hors d'oeuvres and tobacco smoke, one might have thought a party was going on in Mrs. Morrow's living room. Only one thing was missing—the laughter. The crowd's, or should I say the audience's, mood was growing more restive by the minute. My performance would not help.

I leaned toward the mirror propped up on the desk and, for at least the tenth time, checked my makeup and straightened my bow tie. My tuxedo felt both too baggy around my midsection and too constricting around the neck. Either my imagination was playing games with me or my body had radically changed shape in the last few days. Magic, right?

For want of something better to do, I again reviewed the stage cue sheet. The cue at the top of the page indicated that at eight sharp Joyce was supposed to pop her head inside the door and merrily chime, "Full house. Fifteen minutes." Things were behind schedule already.

At 8:06 she stuck her head in.

"Eight-oh-six. Get your ass in gear," she said. She was not merry. She did not chime.

178

"Close enough," I said.

Joyce's pink blouse had cuffs more ruffled than my tux shirt. The blouse's puffiness abruptly tapered in at her waist to a wide leather belt whose buckle was in the design of a sunburst. Her midcalf-length skirt was a muted plaid.

She scanned the paper on the clipboard. "Everyone's here."

"Great. Who was the last to arrive?"

"Fetterman."

"Anyone show up that isn't on the list?"

"Three men. All with Fetterman. All cops, no doubt."

"Wonderful. I feel more secure already. Don't you? Do the coats on Fetterman's men bulge much?"

"I didn't notice," she said.

"It doesn't make any difference. I think it's been five years since they last manufactured bulletproof tuxedos."

She did not crack a smile. The show wasn't out of the dressing room yet, and I was already bombing.

"Tell Mr. G. to start the music."

She nodded.

"Hey," I said. "Don't I even get a—"

She put an arm around me and gave me a short, hot kiss.

"Ouch," she said when her clipboard became trapped between us. She managed to smile, albeit a small one. Then she left to tell Aldo to strike up the band. Or should I say, strike up the tape?

My butterflies had turned into pterodactyls.

Gastini had insisted on using "The Sorcerer's Apprentice" for the opening. I did not argue. Musical choices were the least of my concerns. I did suggest to Gastini that it was too downbeat for an opening number and that people always associated it with the Mickey Mouse cartoon. He agreed, but defended his choice for "symbolic reasons." It left me wondering if he still considered me an apprentice. But weren't we all apprentices at what we were attempting tonight?

The hallway leading from the study was dark. After patting the walls in a fruitless search for the light switch, I took tiny steps, sliding my fingertips along the wall for guidance. My eyes refused to adjust to the dimness. By the time I heard the opening strains of "The Sorcerer's Apprentice," I had positioned myself in front of the doorway frame we had constructed in the middle of the stage.

On precisely the last note of the piece, a flashpot ignited in front of me, stage spots were thrown on, and, by means of a three-thousand-dollar contraption made mostly of wood, felt, and metal brackets, I made my magical appearance in a seemingly empty doorway in center stage.

We had, by rigging portable theatre lighting, hanging makeshift curtains, and slapping lumber together, turned a perfectly good living room into a temporary stage overnight. It would serve our purposes well, the least of which was entertainment.

After the smoke from the flashpot had settled down to a four-inch blanket on the platform, I delivered my traditional opening line.

"Greetings. I am Colderwood. I fool people."

Right on cue, a girl in tights and a skimpy, spangled majorette costume glided out onstage carrying a silver platter. After she showed that it was empty, I passed my fingers over it. Flames belched up from the platter. I passed my hands through the midst of the fire, and it was instantly extinguished. In its place was a fat, white duck that even quacked on command. I was glad that Aldo Gastini had brought a vanload of his apparatus and livestock. The majorette was one of his granddaughters.

The audience, unsure how to react, responded with feeble applause. They had all been invited to the Morrow house tonight without explanation. They were simply informed that their presence was vital.

As the assistant padded offstage, lugging the plateful of live duck, someone in the audience let loose with a catcall.

"We're here to see a goddam magic show? I'm leaving."

The lights blinded me from seeing who was doing the grumbling. Only the front row was visible, and just barely. I recognized Joyce, Mrs. Morrow, and Dr. Randy Pescatore, the psychiatrist, but no one else.

I addressed the faceless heckler.

"Please, take your seat again. I promise, you won't be disappointed. Your time will not be wasted. All of you who were invited here this evening are aware of the confusion surrounding the death of L. Dean Morrow. All of you have some personal stake in learning what the truth is. Tonight you will learn that truth. But you must bear with me. As I said in the beginning, magic is my profession. It's what I do best. Tonight you will learn the truth behind this strange story, but it will be in the form of a—"

"A goddam magic show!"

The audience snickered. I still could not recognize the heckler's voice. But at least he had a sense of humor. And at least he was staying.

"Correction," I said. "The best goddam magic show you've ever seen! Cue number two, Aldo."

Discordant music from the *Psycho* soundtrack filled the room. Flashpots ignited on both sides of the stage, alternating to create a strobe effect. I vanished in a billow of smoke. The applause was stronger this time, but still tentative.

Pep rally fanfare music blared next from the P.A. It almost did its job of covering up the clomping on the stage as the assistants set the next illusion.

Backstage, huddled over a desk in the corner, was Aldo Gastini. He wore a floppy-brimmed black fedora. He still sported the same close-cropped white beard he had when I first met him almost two decades ago. He held a tape cassette underneath the desk lamp, trying to read the label. His eyeglass lenses were so thick they made his eyes look twice their size.

"Fucking tape," he said to himself. "More trouble than live music. Doesn't anyone take music lessons anymore? Unions. That's the trouble. Damn unions."

He shot me a glance that brimmed with distaste. "You! Are you going to persist in deviating from the script? 'Cue number two, Aldo.' Why don't you just pass out a copy of the light and sound cue sheet to the audience and let them call out the cues?"

"Sorry, Aldo. I forgot my line." I pulled his hat down over his eyes. "Better get prepared for more little gaffes. We're not ready for Broadway yet."

He wanted to lecture me further, but the music faded— my cue to go back onstage to begin a lecture, of sorts, of my own.

I snatched up the torch from the prop table, lit it with a cigarette lighter and strode back out through a part in the curtain that the assistants held for me.

"Torch? What torch?" I said. I looked to my left and, just as I was about to look right, tossed the burning stick out into the middle of the audience. It disappeared before it landed. The audience stirred with the nervous laughter I expected.

"How did I do that? I can't tell you. Magicians don't reveal the secrets of their illusions.

"But it's that very subject of reality and illusion that draws us here tonight. The demise of L. Dean Morrow has been shrouded in deception and illusion. Some say he chose his fate. Others say it was an accident. And some believe that he was deliberately pushed off that ledge.

"His widow hired me to clear the air once and for all. For a while I thought I was failing miserably in my task, but tonight is the culmination of my investigation. Incidentally, in case I am accused of venal motives, I must inform you that I have borne much of the cost of the production you are witnessing. My total earnings after expenses will be zero dollars.

"For those of you who know nothing of the conjurer's art, let me assure you that most of the effects and illusions performed by the world's greatest magicians are based on very simple and uncomplicated secrets. In trying to come up with complicated explanations, most people fail to detect the direct and simple solutions to the puzzles they see onstage.

"The death of Mr. Morrow was much the same, except that there were more pieces to this puzzle to agonize over. And there was more than one illusionist responsible for the fog we were all wandering in."

The audience was mine now. No more coughing, rustling, or under-the-breath bitching.

"The time has come to expose—oh, how I shudder at that word—the first illusionist. He is the one who initially drew me into this affair. He posed as L. Dean Morrow and hired me to investigate alleged poltergeists that were plaguing him. I never saw this man again. My meeting with him led to my being questioned by the police. It also led to my meeting Mrs. Morrow and then being hired by her."

Gastini's granddaughter handed me a three-foot square of white poster board.

"Who was this imposter?"

I waved my hand over the cardboard. The white gradually gave way to color, vague and dim at first.

"Here is his picture."

The colors brightened and coalesced into a poster-sized photo of the man who posed as Morrow.

"I learned from Mrs. Morrow that her husband had indeed been pestered by spooks. Not real ones, of course. There ain't no such thing. Believe me. It was outside the Morrow bedroom window that I discovered the real cause of this haunting. It was a clever combination of wires, threads, fluorescent paint, and sound effects—all the props of a seasoned spook show man. They specifically reminded me of Aldo Gastini, one of the best practitioners of the art the world has ever seen."

Gastini loudly cleared his throat.

"Sorry. Some say that Gastini was one of the top three—"

More throat clearing.

"All right. Gastini was *unequivocally* the best spook show man in the whole country. Tonight he is here, but operating in an offstage capacity. I—what?"

What was the audience snickering at? I turned and found myself face-to-face with a floating handkerchief. It was pure white and knotted at the top. The knot wiggled a wave at me. No one, except perhaps the Blackstones, could imbue a floating handkerchief with more personality than Gastini. The hank took a snappy bow, then bobbed and pixilated its way offstage.

"Not for one moment did I suspect that Aldo himself was involved in the harassment of Morrow. He is as harmless as that dancing handkerchief he just paraded by. Besides, the old man doesn't have that much imagination."

The handkerchief zipped back for a quick curtain call, circled me once, and took a dive-bombing swoop at my face. I swatted, but missed it by a foot. It flew back offstage.

"Aldo Gastini told me that he did have a young man assisting him until a year ago. He said this fellow's capacity to learn quickly was miraculous. He was a conjuring prodigy and had learned nearly all that Gastini could teach him. The young man suddenly quit, with no explanation given. His name is Peter Fryer. Fryer's parents are present this evening. They told me that he had always been obsessed with the magical arts. He was a fan of mine and even wrote me some letters years ago. He had ample knowledge and skill to bring to life the ghosts that vexed Morrow."

Sergeant Fetterman's voice interrupted me.

"Where is he now?"

"I don't know. Since his initial contact with me, I have not heard from him. However, I can make a pretty good guess."

"Why would Fryer want to harass Mr. Morrow with that spook stuff?" a female voice asked.

"Who said that?"

Gastini kicked on the lights that were focused on the audience. Instantly, every face in the small crowd was recognizable.

"Who asked that question?"

Donna Smith, the sister of Louise Fasick, the woman Morrow had deserted more than two decades ago, raised her hand.

"That's an excellent question. To which I have a less than excellent answer. In fact, the answer is downright repellent. You really don't know, do you? I would have expected you to figure it out by now. I am quite certain that if matters had been allowed to continue, Morrow himself would have discovered the truth. You see, Peter Fryer is actually Morrow's son."

I explained to the audience how Morrow, as a young man, had briefly lived in Somerset and had unknowingly fathered a child.

"Then my sister really didn't kill her baby?"

"No, she didn't. But she felt as guilty as if she actually had. What really happened was that she abandoned her son. She left him on a doorstep like a sack of garbage, not even checking back to see if the little boy was properly cared for. She transferred to the baby all her rage over her abandonment by Morrow. She spent her last days torturing herself with guilt. She tried to deny the baby's very existence. Figuratively, she killed the child by erasing him from her life.

"Not long after the baby was adopted, the authorities stopped trying to trace its origin. When I talked to Mr. and Mrs. Fryer— Where are you? Oh, over there. They told me how in recent years Peter had become obsessed with finding out who his original parents were. I'm sure it wasn't difficult, once he put his mind to it, to track down L. Dean Morrow as his father. It only took me a couple of days, starting at the other end of the trail, to discover Peter's identity. We magicians have a penchant for finding answers to baffling questions.

"Apparently the facts that Peter uncovered overwhelmed him more than he expected. Instead of simply coming forward and identifying himself to Morrow, he plotted to harass and terrorize him. Perhaps it had been a severe shock for Peter to find out that his biological mother had abandoned him and then committed suicide. He may have loaded the entire blame for her death on Morrow. When we find Peter, we'll ask him. Dr. Pescatore here would be the best man to ask the questions."

The psychiatrist was sitting next to Mrs. Morrow. He seemed agitated by the whole proceedings this evening, and pulling him into the limelight made him more uncomfortable.

"Regardless of his original motives, however, Peter had an obvious change of heart. He ceased bothering Morrow with the fake spooks that Gastini had taught him so well to bring to life. But he didn't have the nerve to come clean to Morrow. He needed help, and I was the one that happened to be nearby. He posed as Morrow and hired me to investigate the hauntings, knowing that with my own magic background I would immediately smell a rat. Fryer hoped I would eventually unravel his whole scheme so that he wouldn't be forced to confront Morrow with the truth all by himself. No such luck. Morrow's death aborted his whole plan. A paper found in Morrow's pocket showed that he had intended to show up at that intersection that night. Peter undoubtedly gave him that message anonymously. If Morrow had been allowed to live, I would have been well on my way to finding the truth of the situation.

"By the way, we took a phone survey of all the motels in the area. At the Berkshire Motor Lodge, out on Route 36, there is a guest registered under the name of L. Dean Morrow, Jr."

One of Fetterman's men gave him a tense glance. He clearly wanted to move out. Fetterman patted him on the shoulder, as though he were an overanxious puppy that needed calming.

Donna Smith spoke up again. "Fryer didn't act in time, did he? Morrow killed himself."

"Actually, you are only half right. Fryer was too late. But Morrow did *not* commit suicide. He was murdered."

"A son killed his own father?" Mr. Fryer said with incredulity.

"No. Not at all. Peter may be a troubled young man, but he did not commit murder. He was well on his way to finding his own path to righting the wrongs he had done. Someone tried to kill Joyce Gildea and me by running us off the road a few days ago. Peter had no motive for doing something like that. No, Morrow was killed by someone else."

I took a deep breath and made sure the apparatus was in place.

"And that someone else was *you,* Logan Zoller."

I pointed my finger at Zoller. A flash of fire was supposed to explode from my finger. Nothing happened. Just as well. It was Gastini's idea, and effective or not, I thought it a bit too much.

I cleared my throat and repeated my last statement. The houselights did not come on full as they were supposed to.

"Light cue, please."

"I was waiting for the fire from your finger," Gastini said from backstage.

"The damn thing won't work."

"Not my fault."

The houselights finally came up.

Zoller sat well back in his seat, exhibiting a calm, easy smile. He blinked slightly from the bright lights that were thrown on him. Even I did not think he looked the least bit guilty.

CHAPTER THIRTY-FIVE

The roomful of people buzzed in conversation, but I focused all my attention on Zoller. I patiently waited until he had finished all his squinting under the lights. When he realized I was waiting for him to respond first, he straightened his tie and sat closer to the edge of his seat.

"Why would I . . . ," he started to say, but the audience was still too noisy for him to be heard. They quickly resettled into silence when he attempted to speak again.

"Why in hell would I want to kill Morrow?" he said.

"In a word: money."

"What money? He left it all to his widow. I got next to nothing."

"The money from the book business."

"You're dreaming, mister. Check our records anytime you want. Editions was nothing more than an expensive hobby of Morrow's. It is hardly worth murdering for. I will make a living from it, but that's all."

"I'm not talking about the shop. I'm talking about *your* book business, the one you run undercover."

Two assistants wheeled a box onstage that was made of hard, transparent plastic. They spun it in a circle so that all could see it was empty.

"What took so long?" I said to one of Gastini's granddaughters in a whisper.

"He wouldn't take his hat off."

"Figures."

We stretched out between us a ten-foot square of silk with a Chinese dragon printed on both sides. We draped the box with it. As we spun the cabinet on its casters, a furious rendition of "Flight of the Bumblebee" poured from the P.A. speakers.

"I thought 'Sabre Dance' was scheduled for this segment," I whispered.

"Grandpop's mad."

"No shit."

We stepped away from the box and clapped once in unison. The music reached a crescendo as I whipped away the cloth to reveal that the box was now filled to the brim with a man. The assistant removed the lid.

The man rose painfully to a standing position, his hand pressed to his lower back for support.

"I was wondering how long you were going to coop me up in there," he said. "I could hardly breathe."

His tweed suit was even more wrinkled now than when we had rehearsed the illusion earlier in the day. He still wore his porkpie hat, which he held in place with one hand while the assistants helped him step out of the box. It was the same hat he had on the other night at the bookshop. While he massaged the kink out of his back, I observed Zoller closely for any reaction.

None.

"This man has agreed to participate tonight because—"

"Agreed to participate? What kind of talk is that? Coerced is more like it," the man said. "You told me that if I took part in this hokum tonight, there was a good chance that I could avoid prosecution when, as you put it, 'the shit came down.'"

"That's close to what I said. We have guaranteed this man anonymity in exchange for his story."

"Some anonymity. Appearing in a plastic box in front of a crowd of people."

He surveyed the audience.

"Holy," he said out of the corner of his mouth. "That guy in the back is a cop. Don't bullshit me. I can almost smell him up here."

"Not only is *he* a cop," I said, loud enough so that only he could hear me, "but so are the two guys on either side of him. Behave and I'll have you out of here before they even think to ask your name.

"Don't worry, folks," I said, piping up again. "My friend's okay. Just a last-minute case of nerves, but he's ready to answer some questions now. Where are you from, sir?"

188

"Amesbury, Massachusetts. Zip code zero-one-nine-one-three."

I was beginning to feel like we were a ventriloquist and his wise-ass dummy.

"Were you at Editions Bookshop two nights ago?"

"Yes."

"What was the purpose of your visit?"

"Why else would I be there? I was buying a book."

"You drove the whole way from Massachusetts just to buy a book?"

"It was a very special book."

"Your hat, please."

"Huh?"

I jerked the hat off his head before he could protest. I do not know why I thought he would be bald, but I was wrong. The hat hid a healthy crop of curly gray hair.

I showed the hat empty and twirled it around on my pointer finger. I reached inside and pulled out a hardbound book.

"Is this the book you bought from Logan Zoller last night?"

He grabbed his hat and peeked inside it before he replaced it on his head.

"The name of the book is *The Eternal Moment* by Forster," I said. "It is a first edition, in good-to-excellent condition. Copyright 1928. Is this the book you bought from Zoller?"

"Yes."

As he reached out for the book, one of the assistants took him by surprise. She draped the cloth over his head. I clapped my hands twice. As the cloth drifted eerily down, the man appeared to melt into the platform floor. I walked over and stomped on the cloth to show that he had actually vanished.

"Regardless of the impression he may have given you, that man is not a professional criminal. He is a perfectly legitimate businessman who owns two package stores and three laundromats."

I hopped up and down a few more times on the cloth.

"We all have our vices. His is rare books. He has been an assiduous collector since he was in his early twenties. He—what?"

I leaped the whole way off the cloth, pretending to feel

something move underneath. The center of the dragon silk bobbed and swelled. The whole square of cloth swayed and rose off the floor. When the center was almost six feet in the air, the two assistants tugged on the edge of the silk and it slipped off the figure underneath.

The man was packed so tightly into his three-piece corduroy suit that he made me feel warm just looking at him. With his arms crossed high at his chest and wearing a pasted-on smile, he was trying too hard to display an air of nonchalance. His forehead glistened, and his moist ringlets of hair clung flat against his ears.

"Good evening," I said. "Glad you dropped in, or should I say 'popped up'? Could you tell everyone your name?"

He wore the other man's porkpie hat. Several sizes too small, it was perched high atop the forest of curls on his head, giving him a Mr. Potato Head look.

"I don't want this damn thing," he said, tossing the hat offstage like a Frisbee. "My name is Willard Hollen."

"Most of you, no doubt, have no idea of who this man is. While most library directors who are faced with budget cutbacks are working day and night, making appearances to appeal for public support, Mr. Hollen prefers to stay close to his office, making sure his ink pad and rubber Yes stamp are in good working order."

"That last remark was unnecessary," he said. "No matter how true it is."

"Mr. Hollen, please remove those papers from your pocket."

"What papers? What are you talking about?"

He checked the inside pockets of his coat, first one side and then the other.

"Nothing here," he said.

With both hands, I traced circles in the air in front of his right pocket.

"Try again," I said.

He reached inside his right coat pocket and withdrew a handful of accordion-folded paper.

"How the heck did you—?"

He partially lost his grip, and six feet of paper cascaded out of his hand before he stopped it.

"Kindly identify that paper for us."

Hollen pretended to scrutinize the document, but succeeded only in dotting it with sweat, not fooling anyone into thinking he was looking at it for the first time. He stepped on the trailing end of the pleated paper and pulled a few more feet of it out of his hands.

"This is a printout from our computer terminal at the library. We primarily use the terminal for interlibrary loan business, and we occasionally use it to tap into a data bank for some of our patrons who are doing research."

"What, specifically, is the content of that printout?"

"It's a listing of all requests for information made from our terminal during the last month."

"Essentially what you have there is a list of book titles along with all the libraries in Pennsylvania that have each book?"

He nodded.

"Unusually long list, isn't it? Do many of your patrons take advantage of your interlibrary loan service?"

"To the best of my knowledge, not very many. My contact with the program is minimal. The librarian that used to run this program is—"

"Dead. Yes, I know. We'll get to that in a minute. Just stop worrying, Mr. Hollen. You are not going to be implicated in any wrongdoing."

He was still edgy over my threat to expose the video bootlegging scheme.

"Now comes the fascinating part," I said, taking another computer tear sheet from my inside pocket. "Here is a printout of all the books that were requested during the past month by the Bayorvale Public Library. Mr. Hollen's list represents requests for information. Mine consists of the actual books that were ultimately sent on loan to Bayorvale."

I let mine unfold. It was only two feet long.

"A bit of a discrepancy, isn't there, ladies and gentlemen? We went one step further and had Mr. Hollen call as many libraries as he could, trying to locate some of the books on his list. How did you do, Mr. Hollen?"

"Not very well. Of the twenty libraries I talked to, eighteen of them could not locate the books I requested."

"Any theories as to why?"

"Some books could be misshelved or in use by other library personnel."

"Is that very likely?"

"Well, it *is* an awfully high percentage."

191

"Could the books in question be in circulation?"

"No. The libraries' records all indicated that the books should be on the shelves. None of the books could be classified as rare, but many are considered scarce. Some are part of special collections and not allowed to circulate under any circumstances."

"What's your estimate of the total value of the books on your list? A wild guess would be sufficient."

"I'd say in the neighborhood of ten to fifteen thousand dollars."

"And that's only for a period of one month. Over a couple of years, that could amount to several hundred thousand dollars. A thrifty man could make that last a lifetime. But then, a thrifty man could live off the proceeds of a moderately successful bookstore and be satisfied, couldn't he?"

"You done with me?" Hollen said.

"Yes. You've been most helpful."

"Is that all you want me to do?"

"Why, uh, yes. Is there something else?"

"Don't I get to leave magically—or something? You want me to just walk off?"

"Sure."

"I thought I'd at least rate a puff of smoke. I—"

He looked down at his wing tip shoes and noticed for the first time that he was floating six inches off the floor. He was as delighted as a kid on his first amusement park ride.

"Hey, thanks," he said, giving me a saluting wave as he floated offstage right, still hovering only a few inches off the floor.

"And now for a short mind-reading segment."

I placed my hand on my forehead and did my best to keep my eye on Zoller.

"I see a basement workshop with many strange tools stored there. For instance, I see many, many different kinds of ink erasers. They would certainly come in handy if one wanted to remove those messy identification stamps that libraries have a tendency to mark up their books with.

"And what's this? Shoe polish? I never knew that shoes came in so many shades. I suppose that you'd need something to cover up the difference in shading on leather bindings once you removed those bothersome stickers some libraries paste on their books. Yep, sure is a lot of shoe polish, particularly when the owner doesn't even take the time to properly shine his own shoes."

Zoller pulled his feet back underneath his chair. He was exhibiting signs of strain in his efforts to retain the passive expression of his face.

"I see magnets. What are they for? No, wait. Ah, yes, now I see. Lots of libraries operate on a security system that senses magnetism. If you carried a bunch of magnets around with you and tripped off a security system often enough when you weren't carrying any books, then when you decided to heist a few books, the librarians would be so used to seeing your face that they wouldn't bother to stop you anymore. Would they, Mr. Zoller?

"You'll have to fill us in later as to exactly what went wrong with your little scheme. I have a few guesses, though. I don't think Morrow ever really suspected that you were running an underground business. But I do think he believed you might be involved somehow in the poltergeists that were pestering him. Whatever the reason, he arranged a meeting with you. Is that why you two were atop that parking garage? Or did you forcibly take him there later? Whatever the case, when he told you that he wanted to talk over something vital with you, you panicked, didn't you? You thought your whole party was over, that he knew you were moving stolen books, using the bookstore as a front. Now you know that you acted too quickly. If you had listened to Morrow long enough to hear about the insane harassment he was enduring, you could have continued your lucrative operation. Maybe he just wanted a friend to confide in, someone to tell the seemingly crazy story that he was being haunted by the ghost of a son he had fathered years before.

"How much are you into them for, Zoller?"

Zoller's only reaction was a flicking blink of his eyes.

"That's what clouded your vision, isn't it? You have a huge debt that keeps growing like a monster. Have you paid much on your principal, or are you just able to make the weekly vig? You must have placed a lot of bets with Fireeno. You have a special button on your home phone reserved just for him. Does he ever call you? Or does he just send his emissaries who are experts, shall we say, in body language? You must be into them for a pile. Enough so that you would send L. Dean Morrow over the railing of the parking garage. How did it happen? Did you push him or did you—"

He moved like a cat. One second he was sitting back, stoically taking all the accusations I slung at him, the next he was only fifteen feet away from me and closing in. The gun in his hand looked like a toy, though I knew it was anything but.

"—or did you force him to jump? I bet you ordered him to stand on the ledge, and then you pushed him. Is that the gun you held on him that night?"

The pistol quivered in his hand. Dammit, I had gone too far. It was not supposed to happen like this at all. He was supposed to break down under the weight of all the evidence and speculation I had built up, and then confess in front of everyone, possibly making a statement or two that could be used against him in court. But now he had other plans.

I dropped flat and rolled sideways just as his pistol made a snapping sound, like a whip.

"Get down," I yelled to the backstage people.

I came out of my roll in a crouched position. I didn't retreat behind the curtain, for fear that he would empty his gun into the backstage area. Zoller seemed momentarily stunned after firing the shot. I wondered if he had ever used the gun before.

"Not the same as running someone off the road, is it? But you had some practice with that. You botched it with Joyce and me, but you did the job right with Dennis Rockwell. I should have realized right away that he was dressed far too well for the kind of money he'd be making as a librarian. He was supplying you with the names of libraries all over the East that had exactly the books your customers were requesting, wasn't he? I bet you saw him talking to us in the library. I didn't think you would miss the used-book sale they were holding that day. You couldn't have known we were just getting routine information from him. Did you think he was talking to save his own neck, informing on your operation? Couldn't take a chance, could you? So you did what you did best. You made it look like an accident."

His grip tightened again on the pistol, but I was rolling long before he popped off another shot. It was not as wild as the first. When I stopped rolling, I stayed flat on my belly. I

194

saw Fetterman gingerly taking half steps down the aisle behind Zoller.

Audience members, most of whom were crouching between the rows of seats, pivoted their heads when they saw Fetterman make his approach. The gun in the sergeant's hand looked monstrous compared to the little silver one in Zoller's. There was no way that Fetterman could get a shot off without endangering the crowd.

Zoller spun around to see what everyone was gawking at. At the first sight of Fetterman, he fired again. Fetterman dove behind a metal folding chair.

"Drop it before you accidentally hurt someone else, Mr. Zoller," Fetterman said. "Listen. I know they were all accidents, weren't they? You never really wanted to hurt anyone. Colderwood didn't give you much of a chance to tell your side of the story. He talks too fast and too loud, and I don't think he painted a fair picture of you. Why don't we go somewhere quiet and talk? You'd be surprised at how much I can understand."

Zoller's fourth shot pinged off the chair in front of Fetterman. The detective tumbled to the side and out of sight behind a whole row of chairs.

I managed to get a few feet closer to Zoller. The gun no longer trembled in his hand. It looked surprisingly natural, like a hand tool he had used all his life. He scanned the crowd. I have sometimes scanned audiences the same way, only my motive was to find a suitable assistant, a volunteer for the show. Zoller was looking for no volunteer. Quite the opposite. He wanted a hostage.

Joyce.

Where was she? I spotted her only a few feet to the right of Zoller, huddled beside Mrs. Morrow and Dr. Pescatore. When his eyes fell on her, Zoller ceased his scanning. Search over.

He strode arrogantly over to her and jerked her to her feet by her arm.

"No!" I desperately tried to cut the distance between us. But I felt bogged down, like I had more chains and weights fastened around me than when I used to do river escapes.

He wrapped his arm around Joyce's neck, settling the crook of his arm underneath her chin. Half his gun was hidden in her blond hair.

Someone tackled me from behind, but inertia kept my

arms and legs pumping, even after I was flat on my face. It was one of Fetterman's men, and he kept his arms clutched around my legs.

"That's better," Zoller said. "Now we can talk some sense. I'm leaving, and she's going with me."

Zoller took short, backwards steps up the middle aisle, dragging Joyce with him. Fetterman sprang out into the aisle, blocking Zoller's exit. The detective held his gun with both hands, pointing directly at Zoller's head. I could see the steel intensity in Fetterman's eyes as he mentally replayed the possible consequences of pulling the trigger.

But he was as hamstrung as I was. Fetterman openly placed his gun on the floor and held his hands outstretched, fingers splayed. He did not want to spook Zoller.

But someone else did.

A demonic laugh erupted from the P.A. speakers—a slow falsetto chuckle followed by the words "Wipe Out." It was the intro to one of the cheesiest rock records of the sixties. After a brief drum solo, the lead guitar, which can only charitably be described as a combination of Chuck Berry and Duane Eddy, began its interminable twanging.

"Turn that shit off," Zoller said.

Before I could call to Gastini to knock it off, the curtain parted in the middle and out popped two of the cutest dancing handkerchiefs I have ever seen. One was white, and the other maroon. They were both knotted at the top.

They pranced, danced, and cavorted to the music. Sometimes they switched places. Sometimes they touched and danced as partners, never missing a beat. They darted so quickly, they seemed to fill the stage with movement.

"Stop them," Zoller said, pointing his gun at me.

"What do you think I am, a magician?"

The hanks continued their gamboling to the surfing music, each time edging closer to the stage apron. They were hypnotic. All eyes followed their flitting. Zoller momentarily relaxed his grip on Joyce, but when Fetterman took a step toward him, he renewed his squeeze around her neck.

"I said to tell them to stop."

He shot twice at the stage, but I knew he had a better chance of shooting the wind than of hitting the device that made handkerchiefs dance.

Was he out of bullets? Had anyone been counting?

Gastini's voice raged backstage and could be heard over

the blast of the music. "You ain't shooting my kids. Not my babies."

I struggled free of the hold the cop had on my ankles. As I closed in on Zoller, Joyce's eyes widened, and she tried to shake her head no.

Zoller pointed the gun at my face. I was not thinking anymore, just moving. I felt the same way I do when I perform the same trick for the thousandth time, totally detached and almost in a dream state. More a spectator than a participant.

Someone behind me yelled to get down, but it was too late. The gun bobbed in Zoller's hand as he pumped the trigger.

There were no cracks or bangs, though. The Surfaris' guitar twangs drowned out the clicks of the hammer on the empty bullet chamber.

I must have really pissed off Fetterman's partner. No neat tackle this time. He slammed into me with a body block that sent me sprawling into two rows of chairs.

I looked up in time to see Fetterman rushing Zoller. A woman panicked and darted in front of the detective. He artlessly stiff-armed her into the laps of three audience members.

"Get away," Zoller said. But he was not talking to any person. He was talking to the handkerchiefs.

The two cavorting squares of silk had vacated the stage and were approaching in midair, all the while keeping time to the music.

They buzzed close to Zoller's face, and he swatted at them with his gun hand, missing them by a foot.

They closed in again, making pecking motions at his eyes. He let go of Joyce to make a vain attempt to grab them out of the air.

The two circled him like miniature helicopters, spiraling around his neck in increasingly smaller circles.

Zoller shouted, but his voice was too hoarse to be intelligible. His eyes opened wide, but all I could see were the whites. As he pawed at his throat, his tongue plopped out. Like a hatcheted tree, he toppled forward. He was totally motionless, not even breathing.

Fetterman was the first to get to him. "Heart attack," he said to one of his men. "Call an ambulance."

197

"No heart attack," I said, pulling myself to my feet. "Get some scissors. Hurry."

I put my arms around Joyce. She fought back tears, but said she was all right. I felt bruised, but was sure no bones were broken.

"Get those scissors. Now," I said.

Gastini sauntered out onto the center of the stage, displaying a foot-and-a-half-long pair of silver shears in his hand.

"Need these?" he said.

"Get over here. Hustle," I said. "This man's strangling from the invisible thread of your dancing hanks."

Gastini hopped off the stage and walked toward us, moving no faster than a casual stroll.

A chubby hand rested on my shoulder. I turned and faced Homey Hudson, the old man Morrow had played games with in the park.

"Now *that* is what I call a show," he said, showing only the barest hint of a smile.

Surveying the makeshift theatre that Gastini and I had slapped together, I saw that it was beginning to look more and more like a living room again. Most of the audience were still crouching on the floor, still unsure of their safety.

It had to be the furthest away I have ever gotten from a standing ovation.

CHAPTER THIRTY-SIX

After Fetterman concluded his interrogation (he called it a debriefing) I had a chance to gulp in about ten minutes' worth of fresh air while Joyce whisked me over to the editorial offices of the *Dispatch*. It was now 12:30 A.M., and the building was deserted.

Two rows of desks, six in each row, stretched from wall to wall in the big barn of an office. Each desk was equipped with an ashtray, and the whole editorial room had a cigar stink that nothing short of a grenade could eradicate. We sat at the city editor's desk. It was bigger than the rest and had more butts piled up in the ashtray.

She snapped yet one more mini-cassette into her recorder. I had lost count of how many cassettes we had been through. So far, I had not balked. It was all part of the deal. She was getting her exclusive.

"How many cassettes do you have left?"

"Don't worry. We won't run out," she said. "There. All ready to go again?"

"You sure this is just for a series of articles? I mean, you're not putting together one of those quickie paperbacks that you'll stay awake three days and nights writing so it will be on the supermarket bookracks next week?"

"Testing. One, two, three."

She rewound the tape and listened to the playback of her voice.

"Ready? Good," she said, not waiting for my response. "Who was it that beat up on you in your motel room?"

"Turn it off."

She refused, so I hit the button myself.

"Off the record? Okay?"

She reluctantly agreed.

199

"All right," I said. "It was Fetterman that roughed me up. He told me so tonight. He was tossing my room, hoping to find something that didn't jibe with my story. His frustration and general loathing of me got the best of him. He regrets the whole thing now."

She nodded, and, as if it were a grocery list, she put a check mark next to the question on her notepad. She restarted the tape.

"Why did Zoller change the lock on the bookstore?" she said.

"He must have read the news article that I did, the one about the ambulance attendants robbing victims. If you'll remember, nowhere on the list of personal effects in the police report does it mention any keys. Yet, among the personal effects that Zoller returned to Mrs. Morrow there was a set of keys. Apparently Zoller took the set of keys from Morrow before he sent him to his death. He didn't want anyone else to get hold of them and rob the bookstore. But then he must have worried that maybe Morrow had a spare set on him, so he changed the locks anyway."

"Tell me again how Logan Zoller got out of that garage the night he killed Morrow."

"No, dammit. My anwer's the same as it was when you asked me the first time. It's all on the second cassette."

Again I stopped the machine. I switched cassettes and hit the play button. In a minute we listened to my recorded voice answer her question.

"Zoller occasionally used stolen cars when he was running stolen books of exceptionally high value," my voice was saying. "It was a stolen car that he used to run us off the road that day. That same car was in the parking garage the night he killed Morrow."

"So?" Joyce's voice on the tape asked.

"What the hell's wrong with you? Can't you ease up for just one second? Can't you at least say 'Congratulations' or 'Nice job'? Why—"

Joyce immediately stopped the tape, ran it forward a few seconds, and let it play some more.

"—in the what?" her taped voice asked.

"Zoller hid in the car," my voice said. "He forced Morrow off the ledge of the garage, and the cold-blooded bastard unlocked the trunk of the car, crawled in, and lowered it as far as it would go without locking. If he had screwed up and locked himself in the trunk, the whole case would have solved itself. The hours in that cramped position, waiting for the cops to vacate the garage, temporarily threw his back out. That's why he moved so stiffly when I first met him." I sounded so much more energetic on tape than I now felt.

"If you are going to listen to this whole cassette," I said, talking over the recording, "why don't you just rustle up another machine and let one record off the other? That way I can catch about four days of sleep, eliminating the middle man."

She ignored me and started recording on the fresh tape again.

"What about all the lovers that Zoller claimed Mrs. Morrow had?" Joyce said. "What that neighbor lady said about repeatedly seeing a male visitor seems to confirm that story."

"Yes. The description of that lover perfectly fits Dr. Randy Pescatore."

"The psychiatrist?"

"Yes. He saw her frequently. Always professionally, never socially. L. Dean Morrow knew all about it. In fact, he was the one who arranged for Pescatore to help her. The doctor, as he told me when we first met, does make house calls."

"House calls." Joyce pondered over it for a moment. "Agoraphobia. She was afraid to leave the house, right?"

"Exactly. Mrs. Morrow is one of those unfortunate individuals too terrified to venture outside. There was not one neighbor who could remember seeing her outside her home. The only possible way for people like Mrs. Morrow to get help is for the therapist to come to them.

"Pescatore is a very dedicated doctor. He was so concerned about her well-being when he heard about Morrow's death, that he immediately offered to assist her in matters that she would ordinarily have to leave the house for. That's what he was doing at the police station that night."

"And that explains why she didn't go to identify the body."

"Right. Pescatore set the authorities straight on her condition. It also eliminated her immediately as a suspect."

My mental cogs felt worn, but Joyce showed no signs of flagging. Every one of my responses seemed to inspire her with five more questions.

"I still have the key to your apartment," I said. "Would you like it back?"

Her mouth opened, ready to toss out another question, but nothing came out. She shut off the recorder.

"When I haul my gear out, I'll leave the key on the coffee table. All right?"

I gave her no chance to talk. I leaned across the desk and kissed her. The kiss she gave in return was as perfunctory and mechanical as her automatic changing of the cassette tapes. I knew that if I gave her a chance to talk again, it would be just more questions.

Her hunger was just beginning. Mine was sated.

I walked out as fast as I could. I trotted down the stairs outside the editorial room, anxious to breathe the fresh, cold air, not caring that it was a long walk back to Joyce's apartment and that I was underdressed. I did not look back.

A man waited for me outside the *Dispatch* building. He was alternately blowing on his cupped hands and rubbing his fingers together.

"If you're going to make a habit of hanging around buildings at strange hours, better buy yourself a pair of gloves," I said to him.

"Or find another line of work," Dr. Randy Pescatore said. "Being an auto mechanic has always held an attraction for me."

I chuckled. "You could combine the two professions: 'Freddy will have the new brakes on your Chevy in a jiffy. Lie down here on the couch and tell me every detail of your last sexual experience.' "

"The way they're making cars lately, I think I'd have an easier time just sticking to working on people's minds." He blew into his hands again. "Fetterman told me you were over here."

"What's up?"

He shrugged his shoulders.

"You're worried about Peter Fryer, aren't you?" I said.

"They haven't turned him up yet."

"You tried the motel?"

"Yes. L. Dean Morrow, Jr., checked out this morning."

I patted three different pockets in search of a cigarette. Pescatore reached in his coat pocket and withdrew a fresh, unopened pack.

"My brand," I said. "You remembered. You a magician or something?"

"Nope, That's why I'm freezing my ass off right now. If I were a magician, I'd be talking to Fryer right now. Got any ideas on where he is?"

"Yeah. I do. You'll have to drive. I'm on foot. Don't worry about finding a parking space. There's plenty where we're going."

During the short drive to the downtown parking garage, Pescatore reassured me that Mrs. Morrow was in no way adversely affected by the circus I had staged at her home. In some ways it might have even helped her. It had been years since she had been around so many people.

Although he drove cautiously, Pescatore's tires still squealed at every turn as we ascended the tight internal spiral of the parking garage. He turned off his headlights before we reached the top level.

The figure almost escaped my notice in the darkness. He stood as still as the concrete pillars that flanked either side of him.

Pescatore turned off the engine, took a long deep breath, and exhaled. Turning to me, he said, "Your work's all done. Mine's just beginning."

He slid out of the car, shutting the door so lightly that it barely latched. He walked slowly but with self-assurance. I felt myself tense up when he took his place beside the dark figure. If the man wanted to toss Pescatore over the parking garage wall, I could never make it there in time to prevent it.

It took forever before they even began talking. The car windows were rolled up, so I could hear nothing. Finally, Pescatore gave the man a pat on the shoulder. They both relaxed. Pescatore gestured for me to join them. It was then that I realized they were standing in the exact spot the police theorized Morrow was thrown from.

"Harry Colderwood," Pescatore said, "meet one of your biggest fans. Peter Fryer."

I shook Fryer's hand, and it felt hot and wet. He stuffed his hands back into the pockets of his down-filled coat. He had his parka hood tied so tightly under his chin that only his eyes, nose, and mouth were visible. I still recognized him as the young man who had posed as Morrow in the mall restaurant. He looked like a turtle peering timidly out of his shell.

"We have already met," Peter said. "Sort of." Unable to look me in the eye, he stared at his feet.

"Don't worry about it," I said. "You did what you thought you had to do."

"Peter has decided to stick around town for a while," Pescatore said. "He would like to learn more about his natural father."

In addition to receiving your help in resolving some of his emotional problems, I thought.

"That's great. Wish I could stay, too. But you know how it is. I've been turning down offers right and left for the past couple of days, and it's time to move on."

"Must really be an exciting life, skipping all around the country," Pescatore said with no enthusiasm at all.

He took a deep breath that made a whistling noise through his nose. "God, look at that moon! Gorgeous, isn't it?" he said.

"Beautiful," I said, before I even looked at it.

The moon was a sliver of dim silver, almost totally obscured by cloud layers. It hung low in the sky, seemingly only inches above the skeleton ironwork of the hospital tower project a few blocks away.

It took many, many minutes of leaning on the ledge and bracing myself against the gusts of November wind before I began to see anything even remotely beautiful about that moon.

I didn't read anything about the case for days. The wire services picked up Joyce's stories, and most of the papers in the state carried them. I sat at the counter of a diner along Route 22. I began my second cup of coffee and my third rereading of one of her articles. The rented Chevette was parked outside the diner. When I found a way of paying the bill for it, I would return it. I guess.

"Your paper's three days old."

I tried to ignore the man who sat down beside me.

"I can understand that," he said. "I always save papers when my name's in print, Mr. Colderwood."

I lowered the paper to take a look at the man. His grin proudly displayed an expensive job of tooth capping. His hair was either meticulously overstyled or one of the best toupees I have ever seen. He was either an agent or very wealthy. In any case, I concluded he was worth talking to.

"Been trying to locate you for three days. By the way, the car rental agency said they are real interested in you too. I have a job for you. Interested?"

"I'll take it," I said quickly. More quickly than I have ever said anything in my life.

"First of all, let me congratulate you for breaking that case."

"Thanks. This is the first newspaper I've bought since the whole thing. Actually, I've been trying hard to forget about it all."

"Oh, I'm not talking about the Morrow case. Like I said, that paper's three days old. Here's a story from this morning's paper."

I skimmed the clipping he handed me. The headline said: "Man Confesses to Murder After Fifty Years."

The article told how a man—after reading Joyce's story about my investigation of the "ghost" of the murdered barber—actually came forward and confessed to the crime. The man, long since retired, would almost certainly not be prosecuted. Authorities were not certain if they could even come up with the police records on the crime.

"That's what I call a reputation with clout," the man said. "Fifty years of guilt, but *you* are the one to scare him into confessing."

"What's the job you got for me? Shopping malls? I'll do the shows any way you prefer. No hassles. Strictly professional. If it's theme parks you want me to work, that's okay, too, even though it will mean sixty or so shows a week. I think I can get along with the college kids you hire as assistants. I even promise not to get too familiar with the girls."

He shook his head, and I noticed for the first time the sadness welling in his eyes. He was no agent.

I braced myself for the story. I knew it would be one of violence and grief. I also knew there would be some element of the bizarre and the inexplicable. That's why he wanted the services of a magician. *A real magician,* as the youngsters would sometimes call me.

205

I also knew I would snatch at the money as soon as he offered it, except that this time I would double- (no, triple-)
check his story before I got involved.

And this time I would not wind up broke in the end.

COLLECTIONS OF TALES FROM THE MASTERS OF MYSTERY, HORROR AND SUSPENSE

Edited by Carol-Lynn Rössel Waugh, Martin Harry Greenberg and Isaac Asimov

Each volume boasts a list of celebrated authors such as Isaac Asimov, Ray Bradbury, Ron Goulart, Ellery Queen, Dorothy Sayers, Rex Stout and Julian Symons, with an introduction by Isaac Asimov.